# Emerald

## LUCKY WRIGHT

18 17 16 15 14 13 12 11
10 9 8 7 6 5 4 3

# EMERALD

# Emerald

*In fond memory of Mary Ann*

I would like to thank Tim Moyer, Teri Ann Moyer, Susan Moyer, Tyler Moyer, Phyllis Wright and Donna Van Horn, for without their tireless help and support, my dream would have never seen the light of day. I also would like to thank the "Reutepohler girls", Mimi and Gladys, who were my Aunt and Mother, inspiring me from birth.

# ACKNOWLEDGMENTS

Published by Moyer Publishing Group, Inc.; moyerpublishing.com

Cover Design by Teri Ann Moyer, TeriAnnMoyer.com
Cover art by Lucky Wright

Interior Design by Teri Ann Moyer, TeriAnnMoyer.com

# *Contents*

# Chapter One

There was not a breath of wind and a gray mist subdued the colors of the Olympic Rain Forest as the first hint of dawn began. There, in a hollow surrounded by majestic trees, two figures appeared dwarfed by their surroundings. Clad only in a white silk tunic, Cyra stood before Mother Nature, barely visible in the gloom and yes, even shadowed by the tallest blades of grass. Barefoot and hardly six inches tall, she carried a tiny flute, sheathed in a silk scabbard between her wings as she nervously wriggled her toes in the damp moss. Though they were friends for a lifetime it seemed, it was still difficult for Cyra to express her own ideas to one so powerful as Mother Nature. Cyra's silver hair, a telltale sign of her many years as Fairy Princess of the Rain Forest, was braided around her crown and fell to her waist in soft curls. She was still every bit as strong and beautiful as that rainy night long ago when Mother Nature gifted her with the title of Princess. It was on her thirteenth birthday Cyra remembered, the magical moment still fresh in her mind. But now Mother Nature searched into Cyra's anxious gray eyes for a clue to her behavior as the crisp October morning settled around them. She could easily sense something unusual in her manner and noticed a tremble in her lower lip as she fidgeted before her. Cyra cleared her throat to speak, but Mother Nature's voice already filled the silence. "You seem uneasy this morning, Cyra. Are you troubled about something?"

"Oh no . . . Well yes, uh, maybe. I have a favor to ask of you and I guess that is why I seem nervous. It is not my place to ask for such a favor but I must say what I feel, don't you think?" she began. "You crowned me Princess many years ago and it has been such an honor, an honor I would like to share with another. It is not fair that I stay Princess forever. There are other fairies that would be responsible and well suited to be a Princess I believe. Also, I think it would make our clan stronger and more united if they were given a chance to serve you as well."

This was a moment for Cyra when the earth stood still. Mother Nature's intense eyes seemed to trespass into her every thought as she stood before her like the Goddess she was. The quietness was deafening. Cyra wrung her hands together waiting for a response. Eternity passed in a blink of an eye. Cyra felt her heart drop to her toes and she bit into her lower lip. Had she hurt Mother Nature's feelings by suggesting someone else should be Princess? *Pickles!*

Mother Nature had the ability to become as large as the Rain Forest or as small as a blade of grass. She could appear before the fairies and elves like smoke, her green hair and garments blending into the mist. With a wave of her hand, she could evaporate into the surroundings as though she never existed, so it was very humbling to be in her presence.

All of a sudden Mother Nature smiled. It was a generous smile and her face radiated like the sun as she spoke. "That is a noble gesture and one I might expect would come from you, Cyra. You are right in your desire to do this, although I do not want to lose you. You were made to be a Princess I do believe."

Cyra exhaled, not realizing she had been holding her breath. She clucked her tongue and her pointed ears blushed from the praise as she answered, "I'll always be here for you, you must know that."

Mother Nature's eyes closed for a moment, but her soft voice continued, "I know Cyra, you could be no other way. Do you have someone in mind to take your place? You must, and I think I know who. Your friend Emerald, am I right?"

"Yes, yes," Cyra squealed. "She would make a perfect Princess, I know it."

Mother Nature tapped her pursed lips with the pad of her finger, thoughts beginning to form in her mind. Troubling thoughts. "She seems to have difficulty focusing, which could be a problem," she answered, placing a rose petal in Cyra's hair." I know that is not entirely her fault," she whispered. "After all, she was raised by elves. They did take her in as an infant and bless them for that. Such a tragedy, her parents killed in that logging accident. But to tell you the truth, she missed most her training on how to be a fairy, having to grow up in the elves' tree house. The elves did remarkably well in so many ways and I don't mean to sound disrespectful, but they couldn't teach her much on how to be a fairy, or even the finer points of flying. Of course, how could they?" I notice she kind of flies now after all your help, but to watch her is sometimes most scary. You've really been her only mother."

Laying a hand on Mother Nature's shoulder, Cyra whispered, "She has heart. More than anyone I know and that is what will carry her through. She might have a little catching up to do fairy -wise, but I'll be there for her. I'll not let her fall." A broad smile broke across Mother Nature's face and Cyra relaxed her posture knowing her idea was accepted by the Goddess of the Forest. This was going to be some surprise to Emerald and the perfect gift for her thirteenth birthday. "Oh my goodness," Cyra sighed, "her birthday is tomorrow. Would it be possible to crown her tomorrow?"

"Why of course. You have everyone here at first light." With those words, Mother Nature blended into a shaft of sunlight and was gone.

Dancing pirouettes on a toad stool, Cyra sang out with joy. Only one lonely soul watched with bored curiosity at Cyra's actions of delight, a very old, grumpy owl named Ma, whose passion it was to know everyone's business. From her perch high in a tree, she swung her head in almost a full arc, the bones in her neck popping like a fast drum roll. She straightened her spectacles with the tip of her wing and then flew silently into the dark forest unseen by Cyra.

*Chapter Two*

Cyra, you can't be serious, though I'm flattered you would choose me . . . And you say Mother Nature thought it a good idea?"

High above the forest floor in the Tree Castle of the Elves, Emerald sat at the edge of her bed, her feet not quite reaching the floor. She thumped her heels against the wooden bed frame in thought as a delicate light washed over their happy faces emanating from a glass prism in the ceiling. "And on my birthday," she began. "*Wow*. But Cyra, I don't know how to be a Princess," Emerald exclaimed. I actually don't know where I fit in. Finding out I was not an elf when I was three was a bit of a shock, but I recovered. This is different though. I don't know if I could ever be a real Princess --- A good one like you."

Cyra sat down beside her friend, hugging her close. "I know you could. You are loved by the clan, the elves, and all the animals, for that matter. I'll teach you everything I've learned, and we'll do it together until you get the hang of it. Tomorrow at first light, we must all be at the clearing in the hollow for the inauguration." Cyra kissed Emerald on the cheek, her face beaming with pleasure, knowing her gift would soon be a reality. She waved at Emerald, as she walked through a tunnel that led to a round portal in the Tree Castle and flew toward her home.

# Chapter Three

It was going to be a joyous celebration in the hollow. The small clan of fairies and Pixies were anticipating the arrival of their, soon to be, new Princess. Under the direction of a young pixie named Lyric, a small group of pixies were singing a soft hymn, their eyes focused on the arrival of Emerald as the first hint of dawn touched the clearing. Dressed in shades of green except for their pointed red boots and caps with a gold ornament sewn at the top, they appeared smaller than fairies and elves, but large in the form of energy. Lyric's ensemble never missed an event, but the rest of the pixie clan was totally irresponsible and could not be bothered with boring commencement exercises. They were off performing some act of devilishness for sure.

Perched high in a tree near the gathering, Ma, the owl watched Emerald and the elves enter the clearing. Emerald's eyes were on the crowd and most importantly the gleaming green eyes of Mother Nature, when her foot caught a twig. Headfirst she fell into the mulch, her entrance hardly missed by anyone. Ma shook her head at the unsightly spectacle, but Mika, the eldest elf, reached down to help her up, dusting the dirt from her new silk dress, shoes and the wide ribbon laces that tied above her calves.

*"Oh pickles,"* she exclaimed, using her forearm to brush strands of ebony black hair from her dark green eyes. "And right in front of everyone," she whispered to Mika.

"Impressive, Emerald, now you have their full atten-tion," Mika said. Mika's wide grin was contagious, and Emerald had to laugh. Everyone knew her even better than she knew herself, so tripping on a twig should not be a shock at all.  Mika took hold of her hand, sliding his spectacles up the bridge of his nose with the pad of his finger.  His head was bald as a mushroom, but with tufts of hair above his ears resembling white snow drifts.  He was the one who found Emerald barely alive near a fallen tree that tragic morning long ago.  She was only months old, when he picked her up under broken branches and leaves, naming her Emerald.  Mika took on the role of parent nearly thirteen years ago.  She was his daughter now as sure as the sun would rise tomorrow, and his proudest achievement.  "Let us go My Lady, for the clan awaits your presence," Mika spoke in his best regal tone.  Holding her hand, he escorted her with pride toward the center of the hollow to face the rest of the clan and Mother Nature, just as the music ceased.  The silence was causing Emerald's heart to race, and she bit down on her lip as the suspense of the moment swept over her like a cold wind.  *She shivered.*  Emerald had never met Mother Nature, and now standing face to face with the Goddess of the Forest was most frightening.

"Emerald," Mother Nature began, "you have been chosen by your clan to take on the title of Fairy Princess of the Rain Forest."  Mother Nature waited for a response.  There was *none.*  A blank look in Emerald's large green eyes was her only answer.

Emerald could not find her voice as Mother Nature's eyes seemed to draw her into a trance and she blinked to free herself from the effect, as the *Goddess of the Forest* continued.

"This silver flute and pouch of Valla Laun seeds will now be yours."

Emerald heard the words, but they seemed to be part of a strange dream. She blinked again, shaking her head to rid herself from the spell.

"Handle these gifts with care, for both are very magical, and you will undoubtedly witness their power in a moment," Mother Nature was saying, still trying to read the blank look in Emerald's round eyes. Even for *her* it was impossible.

"If used correctly, they will give you the upper hand in fighting evil in whatever cloak it might wear," she continued.

Still unable to speak, Emerald fell to her knees and bowed before Mother Nature, her heart racing like the wings of a hummingbird. The Goddess looked down at her soon to be Princess and a radiant smile broke across her face, for she knew what was about to happen the moment Emerald touched the flute. The knowledge filled her heart with joy, making pink rose petals fall from the sky. They sprinkled over the spectators and grounds, just as the singing began again. The rose petals were a strange phenomenon, but very natural in the presence of Mother Nature. The act was only science to her, but a miracle to those looking on.

Now, Emerald knew she would be expected to say something, something preferably profound, as Mother Nature held out the flute before her. Her brain though, had closed down and shut out the lights! Perfect timing. *"Oh help!,"* she whispered to herself with dismay. Mother Nature's green eyes seemed to glow right through to her very soul. Why was this happening, and now when she really needed a brain? Emerald reached out to accept the gift, *dreading* what would come next. She squeezed her eyes closed, her mouth twisting to one side in a knot as if to lessen the anxiety sweeping through her heart. She felt her fingers touch the flute and . . . *Hoowaaah!* Every fiber of her being became aroused, for the tiny flute was sending the knowledge and power of the entire universe through her body like a tornado. Her pointed ears flushed bright pink. She knew she was surely conspicuous with trembling energy coursing through her veins like lightening, but she could not help herself. She exhaled with a *"whoosh"* so loud, it must have sounded like a primal scream to the inauguration party.

Mother Nature and Cyra smiled watching Emerald deal with her new found ability. Mother Nature whispered to Cyra "She will be a good Princess. The magic only works on those with the purest of hearts and . . . Look at her ears. They seem to glow pink and look at all the sparkles floating from her wings. That is a sure sign."

Emerald turned and faced her clan as they clapped and cheered. She held up a hand, not even knowing why, and a hush fell over the hollow that was complete, for not even a mouse dared breathe for a moment or two. It took those few quiet moments for her to realize she was in control of everyone. She looked at her raised hand as if it alone possessed some strange magical ability. Emerald opened her mouth just to say thank you and all at once she was flooded with ideas and things to say. Actually, she could hardly contain herself. The words poured over her lips like water over stones in a brook.

# EMERALD

*You bestowed me with your magic*

*To help you with your cause*

*I shall wisely use these gifts with care*

*To uphold your sovereign laws*

*I will help the smallest plant that grows*

*To the tallest stately tree*

*I'll befriend the creatures living 'neath*

*Your emerald canopy*

*The trees above give right to pass*

*Silver shafts of pastel light*

*Translucent pathways from above*

*That warm the morning bright*

*Your sun is like a kindled fire*

*On a cold and wintry night*

*It falls softly on my shoulders*

*Warms me with its perfect light*

*Sun touches raindrops left behind*

*Storms maddened rage through night*

*How still they rest on leaves and plants*

*While waiting for the light*

*Then they sparkle, dance and play for all*
*An electric wondrous sight*
*Their life ends quick, but in that time*
*Their beauty shines through bright*

*The air is crisp and fresh to breath*
*Rain bathed the forest clean*
*Its beauty is majestic*
*Its beauty is pristine*
*Your forest is like a painting*
*A remembered perfect dream*
*With light and shadows caught in time*
*A pallet of every green*

*Thank you, Mother Nature,*
*You touch my soul, my heart*
*Thank you for this forest;*
*Your most beautiful work of art*

# *Chapter Four*

It was late afternoon and dismal under dark rain clouds as Jamie Larson left school located at the very edge of the forest and headed home. Funny, how the morning started with such a *bang,* his spirits soaring high only to fall flat as a pancake. Hurray, he was now a teenager was his first thought upon awaking; a condition taking a lifetime to achieve. The events of the morning scrolled through his brain as he kicked a stone from the pathway with the toe of his boot. "Happy Birthday," had sounded from the hallway as he struggled to open sleepy eyes. Mothers were the most thoughtful species on the planet Jamie knew. For there she stood in the doorway to his bedroom holding a cupcake with a glowing candle stuck in the icing. Life was good. It did not take long though for the bubble of joy to burst like a water balloon hitting the cement. With school out, Jamie had stood under a willow tree in the courtyard, the perfect time and place it seemed to ask Shawn Leslie to go to the prom. He stood there paralyzed with fear yet knowing he could not put off asking her another day. Why did only a few words spoken to a girl he liked take so much courage to say? But then, her answer came so unexpected, hitting him with the force of a speeding locomotive. "Oh . . . I'm *sorry* Jamie," Shawn said looking him straight in the eyes. "Bobby just asked me to go with him. It was getting so late; I didn't think you would ask me."

Throwing his arms in the air to relieve the sorrow, Jamie shook his head back and forth repeatedly. Why had he put off asking her? *Why? Why?* Jamie pushed back tears in an effort to mask the pain, for now it was too late. Why was he so afraid of girls, particularly Shawn Leslie? She had never been mean or given cause to suggest violence. She was perfect. Inside though, he really knew it was his fault for not asking her sooner. He was his own worst enemy and his lips scrunched to one side as he considered his blight. The prom was his last chance to tell her how he felt, a chance now ruined. So why couldn't he tell her now? *Because he was a chicken and probably one of the reasons she decided to go with Bobby.* "Oh darn, oh darn," he mumbled, kicking another stone from the path. The short walk home along a well-worn bridle path into the forest was something he usually enjoyed though now the gloomy sky matched his disposition. Soon in the distance, blue smoke rose in faint wisps above the chimney of a log cabin nestled in the trees that his dad had built, the smoke being a reminder that a birthday party was being planned in his honor. *You should have asked Shawn over to the party* his mind taunted. *She would have come. Rejection . . . That was what he was afraid of. Rejection was like some big hammer in the sky with the power to crush dreams in a heartbeat like a lowly bug.* "Why am I such a wimp?" Jamie mumbled reaching the porch and throwing his backpack on the stairs. Tense fingers pushed through shoulder length blond hair, his tearful blue eyes staring at the front door. He couldn't face his mother just now. She would sense something wrong and ask questions. This was a problem way too personal for that. A plan began forming in the back of his mind. *A dark plan.* His eyes narrowed. His fingers began tapping nervously on the railing. He would go hunting; a sport his mother would not allow.

Rejection seems to lead one down a path they would ordinarily not consider. This was one of those moments as dark shadows from the trees stretched across the pasture in the last glint of sunlight. Jamie headed for the barn. The heavy doors creaked open, still air attacking his nose with the scent of hay, alfalfa, oats, leather and horse. Jamie headed for the hay, bailed with wire and stacked high in one corner of the barn. Just with the movement of the doors, Jamie could see the dust swirling in the shafts of light coming through the opening from the late evening sun and he squeezed his nose to keep from sneezing. Several bales lay broken open on the floor and he fell to his knees to retrieve a Red Rider Daisy Air Rifle hidden deep under the pile. He was not allowed to have a gun. *"Guns are for killing things"* was his mother's firm words. No matter how much he argued that a gun would be for target practice, she would not budge from her position. "Practice for what? To one day kill something? You don't need a gun. That's final!" she had said, wiping her hands on her apron and storming back into the kitchen. Tommy's parents let him have a gun, a twenty-two caliber. The once coveted air rifle received by mail order years before, he'd now outgrown, so he handed it over to Jamie. Not wanting to go against his mother's wishes, the rifle lay concealed under the hay for months, but now, anger ruled over good judgment. *Anger at himself.* This was bad timing to be making decisions regarding weapons one must admit, but at the moment it made sense to Jamie. Groping in the dark, he wrapped his fingers around the small vial of BB shot, stuffing it in his pocket. He looked through the cracks in the siding of the barn to make sure his mother was not standing on the porch. Then quietly, he ran through the pasture toward the Rain Forest. For now, excitement pushed other problems back and out of reach as he stepped into another world. Deeper and deeper Jamie walked with the stealth of a trapper into the dense forest as maybe Daniel Boone would have done. Occasionally he would shoot at a leaf or rock to test his skill, unaware night was approaching and wind in the trees signaling a storm.

Finally, there it was. A squirrel poised on a branch as if cast in stone and Jamie's heart began to beat like a drum roll as excitement surged through his veins in anticipation. Without thinking, he took aim and squeezed the trigger. *Pop!* The thrill of that first moment turned to sadness watching the squirrel catapult through the air like a broken toy to land in the mulch trying desperately to catch its breath. Sadly, he looked up at Jamie wondering what happened. Then his eyes closed for the last time as life slipped away. His mother's words now had meaning he could understand and he felt sick to his stomach. He had killed another being for no reason that would ever make sense. With tears falling from his eyes, he dug a hole to give the animal a decent burial. *But what if he is still alive* a voice in his head screamed? Maybe he's *just unconscious. To bury him alive would be another sin.* "I'm sorry," Jamie cried, staring down at the lifeless form he alone was responsible for. He threw the rifle into the bushes as though it possessed some wicked mind of its own and tossed the BB's after it. It was then he realized it was almost too dark to see as rain began falling from leaves. Turning for home, it seemed God was provoked with his cruel act, for thunder cracked across the heavens in response. Which way was home though? Everything looked the same now . . . Dark. No point of reference to determine east from west. He picked a direction and started out hoping something would look familiar.

Nothing did. It seemed like hours passed, his clothes now torn and skin bleeding from prickly brushes and branches. Panic crept into the corners of his mind like water through sand. What to do? Going the wrong way would mean lost forever. Wind howled through the trees now, sending driving rain, drenching him to the bone. Teeth chattering, he knew he would not last long if the weather continued with such anger.

Jamie had never prayed. Well, maybe for a bicycle once, but he considered praying was something best left to grownups. Praying always seemed to be tied to a social event like before a Thanksgiving dinner, or before a ball game. Now the idea took on a new tangible meaning. Without help he would surely die, leaving his family to wonder what happened? He began to shake. Was it just nerves or the cold, but then what difference did it make anyway? None! God would be the only one around now that could possibly see or hear him was his final judgment. No one else would be out here for miles in any direction for sure. Jamie fell to his knees sobbing. God was his only chance now.

"God, if you can hear me please listen," Janie began, his lips trembling with emotion. "I think I just killed one of your squirrels and for no reason. I'm so sorry for doing such an act. I promise it will never happen again. Now I'm scared for my own life though not just for me. My parents and little sister will really suffer, and they won't even know what happened. They don't deserve this. My stupid actions are not their fault. I was disobedient by being out here and having a gun in the first place. Please help me through this and I promise to be a better person. You won't be disappointed."

With those words, Jamie pushed himself up off of the wet ground and turned in a circle, searching for what, he wondered? Not much to notice in the dark. *Darn*, was he ever confused. He took off on what he supposed was purely a random choice, for he had no clue to any real direction. At this point in time though, it did not matter a whole lot, for it was out of his hands. Hopefully God listened. Or maybe he would see a remembered landmark. That was not likely to happen though. Another depressing thought that crossed Jamie's troubled mind was . . . Why would God bother to help him, right after he shot one of his squirrels? Jamie shuddered as the cold reality of making poor decisions stared him in the face. *Just keep moving* his mind taunted in a very anxious manner. *That is the only ability you have to work with for now.* He pushed through thick plants and trees sometimes wedged so close together he had to squeeze between them. The going was agonizing with visibility nearly zero. Between being the blackest night, he had ever witnessed and the thick forest, he might as well be in a deep dark cave, his troubled mind suggested. He hurried on, but with each step becoming more and more anxious, knowing he could be going the wrong way.

Finally, Jamie's mind came to the realization that he really had to be going the wrong way or he would have been home by now sitting by a warm fire and opening presents. But just as he turned to try another direction, a strange sound caught his ears. Stopping for a moment, he held his breath to hear more clearly. Why was the sound familiar? *Water!*

It was the same sound he remembered of a brook near his home where the water turned over rocks and pebbles and lapped against itself in constant motion. He hurried in haste toward the sound for no other reason than it was at least a destination. Approaching a clearing, lightening cracked above, resounding through the heavens like a ricocheting cannon ball. In that moment, he was given light to see, for the forest lit up like a football stadium. In that brief moment, there before him like a still black and white photograph caught in time, a small river rushed back through the dark trees to meet the sea somewhere. Directly in his line of vision was a boat lashed to a tree, straining against the fast-moving current. Jamie's heart skipped a beat. Now, at last there was hope. Someone could be aboard, someone who could help. Now pitch black again, he groped his way toward the direction of the boarding plank. "Thank you, God," he muttered as lightening brightened the sky again. This time he caught sight of the faded letters *"Northern Bear,"* barely visible through streaks of rust and chipped paint. He walked carefully up the creaking boarding plank with a glimmer of hope returning to his thoughts. Hope though, faded rapidly for no lights were on and the boat was noticeably in bad repair. Leaves and small branches cluttered the muddy deck, plugging the scuppers, and hindering the rainwater from draining back into the river. His shoes sloshed through the water puddling on the wooden deck. Once brightly varnished handrails and mahogany trim were now left to the elements and reduced to rough and blackened wood. Years of paint work on the cabin sides now stood peeled away like the pages of an old book forgotten on a park bench. The thought "abandoned," made his heart sink like a rock as he reached for the handrail. Banging on the cabin door brought no response while wind and rain lashed out with vengeance against his shoulders, soaking him to the bone. He tried the doorknob. *Locked!* Shuffling along the narrow side deck, it was impossible to see through the dingy glass panes into the dark interior. All the windows were latched but one, opened barely a crack. His heart skipped a beat, but try as he may, with fingers shoved between the window and sill, it would not budge an inch, glued in place by years of paint. Now what he needed was a pry bar. A broken oar on the aft deck in a dilapidated lawn chair with its webbing tangled and blowing in the wind, looked like the perfect tool. With the thin paddle end jammed above the sill, the window opened effortlessly with the increased leverage. At this point survival took over and breaking and entering was not even a question brought to mind. He slid through the opening to land in a ball on the floor.

Dank and musty, the still air lay heavy in the salon, the pungent scent of rotting wood filling Jamie's lungs. His nose began to run. He wiped at it with the back of his hand as he groped for something solid to pull himself upright with. Holding to a countertop, he stood, afraid to move for fear he would fall through a hatch carelessly left open to crash into something very unforgiving to his wellbeing. To add to the problem, it took all his effort to just stay balanced, for the boat lurched against its mooring line like a chained pit bull. With equal intensity, it hammered itself back against the bank with a sickening *"whomp"* as Jamie held on for dear life, his fingers digging into the raised molding around the countertop. *"The good news"*, his mind offered was, *"You're out of the wind and rain."* But the *Northern Bear* creaked and groaned with a voice so real it threatened Jamie's sanity. *Not good.* His heart was surely going to beat a hole through his chest and escape to who knows where? *Calm down* his mind warned, and he took several deep breaths to still his heart when lightening lit the cabin bright as bright. A bunk caught his eye on the far side of the salon and he stumbled forward, pulling himself over the side board. The mattress and blankets, stained from years of use without care were covered with flaky wood, paint and dirt falling from the ceiling, but that was the least of Jamie's problems. They were dry and now he could get warm. Lying still under the soiled blankets, he listened to the sounds of the boat's torment. This was scary! Thoughts of home and family soon filled his mind and he began to see things in a different way. Simple things he had always taken for granted took on a new and deeper meaning. He let his mind wander…

*I've never been alone before*

*I've never been so scared*

*Where I could not call for help and know*

*That someone heard and cared*

*I've had bad dreams, woke frightened of scenes*

*My mom would hold me tight*

*She'd calm my heart and stay with me*

*The room was left in light*

*Alone with fear you have to be*

*To really see things clear*

*To appreciate friends and family*

*I hold them all so dear*

*I miss the fireside glow, the pillowed hearth*

*Air scented with spiced hot cider*

*Fresh baked bread from the oven pulled*

*Silly questions from my sister*

*She was the voice of her muted friends*

*Who came alive when she was there*

*Oh God see me home I pray*

*My family I must show*

*That I really care about them and I miss them so*

*I miss the chair soft as feather down*

*In the center of the room on a brown braided rug*

*Her dolls would be staged with care*

*I would snuggle next to mom*

*She'd read aloud Tom Sawyer*

*Her voice so soft, so calm*

*I'd really like to help her*

*To show her that I care*

*And do the things she asks of me*

*To be close and always fair*

*I miss my dad just home from work*

*Our mom he'd gently kiss*

*He'd hug us all then smile at mom*

*And wink at me and sis*

*My bed would feel real warm and soft*

*Oh, I wish I had the choice*

*To be there now and see my toys*

*And hear my family's voice*

*My family's voice*

# *Chapter Five*

Emerald walked through a tunnel leading off her bedroom to a round open portal above a limb, located high in the elves' Tree Castle. Once outside, she reached to a branch for balance as the tree swayed with a gust of wind. Raindrops touched her bare shoulders leaving no doubt in her mind a storm was building. Something seemed unsettling and she kneeled on the limb, compelled to reach for the silver flute. As she touched the keys, the same rush she experienced in the hollow returned and she felt in tune with the universe again. It was then she sensed a call for help. Not in words or pictures in her mind, but rather a feeling in her heart. *Mother Nature* had given her more than magic. She had opened up some window in her heart that made her a part of every living soul. Someone was in trouble and she must act! She placed the flute back in the scabbard and jumped from the branch just as a flash of wind caught her side. She spiraled toward the ground unable to gain control. Lightening boomed overhead just as she hit the ground as if it was choreographed by nature.

"Gracious," she exclaimed, dusting herself off, undaunted by the small misfortune. She checked her wings to make sure everything was still intact and cleared her throat. Words poured from her mouth again as they did in the hollow without giving it a thought.

*Storm legions march across our land*

*Black soldiers fill the sky*

*This night somewhere the forest dark*

# EMERALD

*I sense a mournful cry*

*I must hurry through this darkness*

*A silence shouts inside my brain*

*I must hurry so the cries called out*

*Have not been called in vain.*


*I will follow my heart, it will show me the way*

*Swiftly I'll soon find the call*

*I will follow my heart it won't let me down*

*There's someone I cannot let fall*


*First drops of rain now kiss my skin*

*Falling softly from branches and leaves*

*Storm's messenger; a cold night wind*

*Grown angry from a dry hot breeze*

*Dragon's head shall rear with spite*

*Breathing lightening wind and rain*

*Cries will fall silent before trees this night*

*Unable to stop the pain*


*I will follow my heart, it will show me the way*

*Swiftly I'll soon find the call*

*I will follow my heart, it won't let me down*

*There's someone I cannot let fall*

Jamie was not aware he had fallen asleep, finding himself tumbling on the floor, his mind desperately trying to make a connection. To understand. What was going on? Why was he so dizzy? Trying to stand would be a useless feat until his brain quit spinning like a top. Thoughts tumbled inside his head. The boat! He was on a boat. Crawling on all fours, he reached the open window again, staring into the night sky. With another flash of lightening, his heart stood still at what he saw. Torn loose from its mooring by the ravaging current, the boat was spinning out of control down the fast-moving river. Jamie climbed through the window and grasped the handrail with both hands. Now he was really in for it. Every time things looked like they couldn't get worse . . . They got worse. It would be impossible to jump and swim to shore. The violent current would whisk him into oblivion like a twig. To stay with the boat conjured up visions of it going over a waterfall and breaking into pieces . . . Some of those pieces being him. Again, there seemed to be no solution. He was a goner.

The *Northern Bear* banged into a huge boulder jutting from the dark frothy river and shuddered like a dog shaking water from its fur. It groaned like some wounded wild beast, as it slid around the boulder to regain its momentum again. Thrown to the deck, Jamie scrambled to get his bearings. As he reached for the railing, he thought he heard a voice. That was impossible. He shook his head violently to clear his brain, but there it was again.

"Jamie . . . Jamie?" Emerald called down from atop the handrail, her arm wrapped around one of the steel pipes protruding through the railing and reaching to support the overhead. This was her first encounter with a human, but hey . . . It was easy enough to see he was in serious trouble. She watched as he tried to focus on her, scrunching his mouth in a funny manner. *Was I transparent to him?*

Jamie banged his forehead with the palm of his hand hoping to clear his brain from images of some sort of fantasy. Did that thing on the railing just speak? Hallucinations usually followed a high fever, not severe fright was his conclusion.

"Jamie, Jamie. Stand up."

"All right, all right" he wheezed. *It did speak,* a voice in his head insisted, *very faint but most pronounced.*

"You . . . You're not real" Jamie choked over the words.

"I answered your prayer," Emerald remarked, staring directly into Jamie's eyes with a new confidence that surprised even herself.

Shaking his head, biting his lip in frustration, he sighed. *Yes, he had prayed* he remembered. But then what he saw next was beyond any rational explanation. A full moon tracking behind black clouds beamed on Emerald's wings for an instant and there were no words to describe a world turned topsy – turvy. Jamie's voice trembled answering the strange vision before him for how could she be real? This moment went against everything he was taught to believe. "Darn" he mumbled. "I'm afraid this boat is going to break up on the rocks or go over falls somewhere very soon," he began. *He personally would be heading for eternity wherever that was.* Eternity was a word he only heard in church occasionally, entering in one ear and escaping out the other. His real focus was always on Shawn Leslie sitting two rows in front of him with her family. It seemed the sun shining through the stained-glass window high on the church wall, would always light her reddish blond hair, making it seem to glow from within. It was difficult to pay heed to a dull sermon with something as appealing as Shawn's hair to distract his attention, but now the word Eternity seemed to hit him between the eyes with a new scary reality. "You're right, I did pray, but I'm afraid nothing short of a miracle like a crane from God is going to help now," Jamie cried, waving his arm in the air as if to say goodbye to the world. "I don't believe in fairies, and even if I did . . . What are you, maybe six inches tall? I don't think you can help even if you do exist, but thanks for the offer." Jamie's lower lip trembled as he spoke, and Emerald could see the fright in his tear-filled eyes as he tried to stand. She faced Jamie with a confidence she didn't question. There was not a thought in her mind that what she was about to attempt would fail.

"Jamie, size is an attitude, not a condition. Also, you must know that to those who cry out in earnest with a true heart, their voices will be heard." Taking a small Valla Laun seed from her pouch, Emerald placed it into the end of the silver flute while noting the stunned look on Jamie's' face from the corner of her eye. *She smiled.* Turning toward shore, she took a deep breath and blew into the other end. A silver cord shot from the flute into the stormy night air like a speeding bullet lighting the sky like a fireworks display on the Fourth of July. The end of the silver cord wrapped around a large branch at the river's edge and melted together tighter than any knot. The other end, she took from the flute and spun it around a cleat on deck until it became one with itself. Emerald sheathed her flute and crossed her arms over her chest as success was about to happen, she knew for a fact. Jamie looked on with incredulous uncertainty.

High in a tree on shore down river from the *Northern Bear*, Cyra looked on ready to spring into action if it became absolutely necessary. This was Emerald's first test as a Princess, and she wanted her to succeed all by herself. She watched as the silver cord took up the slack and the *Northern Bear* now headed for shore like a mad bull. Cyra covered her eyes and peeped through her fingers as the boat slammed into a boulder at the riverbank with a groan that echoed through the forest like a train wreck, close and personal. Jamie was thrown to the deck disoriented. Emerald though, wasn't quite so lucky. She tumbled off the railing with her arms still crossed over   her chest, a smile still on her lips. But no sooner had she hit the   water than she scrambled up the side of the boat to take her place on the railing, trying her best to look like nothing happened. Smoothing the hair away from her eyes, she was glad to notice Jamie was unaware she fell. That was good. A Princess should have been aware the boat would come to an abrupt stop. *Remember to focus on all the possibilities next time* her brain shouted. Cyra breathed deep seeing how well the magic and Emerald's ability had worked together and without any interference from her or Mother Nature. She was proud of her friend. She turned for home knowing the forest was in good hands.

# Chapter Six

Charred embers glowed dim above the grate in the main room of the log cabin, giving off the scent of pine. On a wooden table, thirteen candles stood like soldiers at attention, ankle deep in vanilla icing atop a birthday cake yet to be served. Ken and Laura Larson sat quietly, waiting for their ten-year-old daughter Amy to speak. She shuffled her feet under the chair, holding tears back. "Mother, I did see Jamie run from the barn into the forest and he did have a rifle. It was late afternoon."

"Jamie doesn't own a gun. Guns are forbidden, he knows that," Laura's voice trembled.

"Tommy got a new rifle and he gave his old one to Jamie. It was hidden in the barn. He knew he was not supposed to have it."

"And you watched your dad search the barn and grounds for Jamie for nearly two hours and didn't open your mouth?," Laura exclaimed with fury. Her hands trembled as she wadded and smoothed her apron on her lap in frustration. *"Oh my God!"*.

"I thought he would show up any minute and I would not have to tattle," cried Amy. "Now I'm really scared." Amy hid her tears behind a dinner napkin, sobbing, "I'm sorry, Mom."

Ken reached across the table, laying his hand on Amy's shoulder. "Amy . . . You were trying to protect your brother and that is a good quality. It is not your fault."

"He could be in danger and I could have helped by telling you where he was."

"You did what you thought right at the time, Amy. We must make choices sometimes at a moment's notice in our lives; there is no way around it. When we look back over our decisions, we might see where we made a mistake in judgment. That's how we learn. We don't need to find someone to blame, we just need to go find Jamie. So don't cry . . . We'll find him, I promise." Ken pushed away from the table, the chair legs grating over the wood floor. He set his napkin on an empty plate and cleared his throat. "Let's get rain gear together and dress warm, guys. Amy, find all the flashlights and I'll dig up batteries. Laura, put together a snack and we'll get going. We better leave a note on the table for Jamie to stay put if he shows up. We don't want to have to look for him twice. Being night and the worst storm ever, don't be surprised if we don't find him right away. I'm sure we will by dawn. He hasn't had time to get too far away".

Only minutes passed before the Larson's crossed the pasture and headed into the dense forest, flashlight's beams bouncing a random pattern before them. Dragging his whole family out in such weather was a necessity now, but he worried about the pitfalls of such an act. He concealed his uneasiness by focusing on the problem.

\*\*\*

Emerald kneeled next to a giant. Her six-inch stature was shorter than the length of Jamie's hand. Having the ability to save Jamie's life swelled her heart, but what to do with him now?  She couldn't just leave him alone to fend for himself, that hadn't worked very well so far.  Emerald reached over her shoulder, her fingers touching the flute and the rush returned.  Even the impossible now seemed within reach, grand ideas exploding inside her head like fireworks.  She took a couple deep breaths to calm her heart.  *Why not make him small like you* a voice in her brain suggested?  *Just for the night until the storm is over.*  The thought rolled around in her head and started to make real sense.  Once smaller, she would not have to worry about being stepped on and she could take him home to a warm tree castle.  Tomorrow at first light she could zap him back to size for his family to find.  *He must have family* she pondered, *and they are probably worried sick wondering what happened to him.*  She watched Jamie, his eyes transfixed on the Northern Bear as it groaned for the last time and sunk below the dark raging river to a watery grave.

Jamie closed his eyes in disbelief then turned toward Emerald.  His idea of what the world was really like was going to have to change or he would have to wake up.  *Soon!*

Jamie . . . Is someone looking for you?" asked Emerald.

"I'm sure my parents and sister are by now, but they don't know where to look."

"They will figure it out, but until then I have a plan." Emerald took a Valla Laun seed from her pouch and pulled the silver flute from its scabbard.  "I want to make you small like me.  Would you mind?  That way you would fit in our *Tree Castle* and we could get you warm.  Look at you. You're shaking like a leaf."

"I cannot believe this for a moment" he sighed, blinking his eyes to get them to work properly. It is not physically possible for you to pull off such an event, but even if you could. . . I'm liable to stay that way." Jamie held his head down, brushing the palms of his hands over his wet hair in total frustration. *Why could he not wake up? This could not really be happening. Could it?*

"I wouldn't leave you like that. You have to be normal when your family finds you and they will. Why do you keep blinking your eyes and staring at me? I'm beginning to feel self-conscious."

"Pardon me, I don't mean to be rude. I guess I was staring, but I keep thinking my mind is playing tricks on me. I can't believe you are real."

"Emotion unlocked our world to you. It doesn't happen often, but enough to have your story books filled with tales about fairies. Think about it Jamie. Those pictures originally began when someone had an experience much like you are having now." Emerald could almost see the wheels turning in Jamie's head as he tried to make sense out of what seemed pure fantasy. If this was a dream, then he would soon wake up from some point where the dream started. Where would that be? He had no clue. To perform a stunt like she was suggesting seemed impossible. No one could have that kind of power. So Jamie's conclusion was to play it out and call her bluff. One thing for sure though, it was good to have company, even if it was just his imagination. Jamie tapped the pad of his finger against pursed lips. "Is this going to hurt?"

Emerald laughed and caused a smile to break through on Jamie's face.

"Of course not," she mused. You'll probably feel better than you ever have in your whole life."

"Okay, I'm for it, Jamie wheezed, his throat suddenly feeling coated with gravel. What were the options staring him in the face? *Exactly none.*

Emerald flew over and landed on her new-found giant. She placed a Valla Laun seed in his shirt pocket and stared into his bewildered eyes that now seemed frightening and enormous at such a close range. *Oh my gosh!* But with flute in hand, she scrunched her mouth to one side ready to do the impossible.

"The light will be intense, so close your eyes and hold your breath. You'll feel a warm and fuzzy feeling for a moment and then you'll be small like me. Ready?"

"Do it," Jamie replied with eyes closed, his body rigid as a steel rod like one would expect from a person's demeanor flying down the steepest track in an amusement park, strapped in a roller coaster.

Emerald thought about what she wanted to happen then touched the flute to Jamie's chest over his heart. Immediately he was enveloped in a silver light that sparked into the sky turning night into day for a brief moment. Jamie was afraid to open his eyes. He'd felt the blinding light clear through his closed lids, a whirring feeling inside his heart and yes . . . all of a sudden, he was warm and fuzzy.

"Jamie, open your eyes. Jamie? . . . Jamie?"

Jamie's heart was trying to pound itself free. Never had he been plain scared just to open his eyes before. Well, maybe once during a horror movie, but this was different. *Blithers!*

"Jamie, will you please open your eyes and look around? You have nothing to fear, I promise."

With much effort, Jamie opened his eyes and, in that instant, his fears subsided and there he was, six inches tall for sure, because Emerald stood over him exactly the same size with this incredible grin on her face as if to say, "*told you so.*" Jamie could really see her now in every detail, down to the sparkle in her eyes. She was beautiful.

"What do you think, Jamie? You look much better now that you're not so monstrous. I'm impressed."

Jamie looked over his body. Gosh, even his clothes still fit. "How did you do that?"

"It is an ability given me by Mother Nature, but I have no idea how it works. I just know it does."

The wind began howling again through the trees, pushing the driving rain sideways when Emerald took Jamie's hand. "We must hurry. We have quite a distance to travel and it is not going to be easy in this weather. Are you ready? We'll have time to talk when we're warm and in the *Tree Castle.*"

Jamie's world had turned topsy-turvy going against all the rules that intelligent people spoke of as fact. The good part though, was for some reason or maybe beyond reason . . . Emerald made him feel safe in this forest that nearly took his life.

"Let's go. If I start moving, I might get warm. Part of my shaking I think is nervousness. I was really scared."

"Everything will work out for you Jamie . . . I promise."

Jamie followed Emerald through the dark forest, amazed at how huge everything seemed now. Water pooling from the rain was a danger. Having to skirt around a large mushroom was even comical and gusts of wind would often throw them off balance. To Jamie though, this was a walk in the park after the boat ride. So far, the whole night was like a page out of "Alice in Wonderland." But oddly enough, just like Alice, he was now able to take it in stride for some strange reason.

Ma, the owl, watched from her perch high up in a tree. She had to squint as she busied herself cleaning the rainwater off her spectacles with a corner of the kerchief tied around her neck. She shook her head in disbelief. *Why would Emerald bother?* Humans were not a trustworthy bunch. She looked away in disgust.

* * *

In another part of the forest, lights flashed back and forth between the trees like huge fireflies out of control. "Jamie . . . Jamie . . . Jamie," began a chorus of three different voices behind the source. Ken was getting hoarse and so far their yelling had produced nothing.  No Jamie.  But in reality, he knew it would probably be more like morning before they stood a good chance of finding their son.  Anxiety threatened to rule his emotions, but he knew he must appear calm before his wife and daughter.  Why did this have to happen on the worst night in history?  Animals were enough of a danger without adding wind, rain and cold to the mix.  His mind wandered to the many camping trips spent in the forest with his family.  He had taught them well about the need for survival.  Jamie was a good student in learning the ways of the forest.  Ken was grateful for that.  Barring some incident that was really crazy, he would probably be fine.  There were a lot more dangerous places to be in than a forest.  Still, concern gnawed at the edges of his sanity like a hungry rodent.

"I'm getting scared, Ken," cried Laura holding tight to his hand.  Amy's hand was locked around the waist belt of Laura's heavy jacket, not wanting to be lost in the blackest night ever.

"Jamie is pretty savvy when it comes to survival.  He should be okay on his own, but we'll find him, Laura.  It might be morning, but we'll find him.

"Maybe a bear will find him first," Amy added.

"Don't you ever say things like that or even think them. *Not ever"* demanded Laura, tugging at her daughter's arm

"Not to worry.  Bears and most animals would not be out looking for food or trouble on a night like this," Ken offered, hoping to settle his wife's frizzed nerves.

"Just the same, that was a cruel thing to suggest," Laura warned, her eyes narrowed toward her daughter, lips pursed shut.

# Chapter Seven

Jamie followed Emerald fairly close, panting heavily from near exhaustion but refusing to give in, not wanting to look like a wimp in the eyes of his new friend. It seemed they'd been running forever, but then how much ground can you cover when your six inches tall? It would take forever to travel any distance at all. With his mind spinning around thoughts of this nature, he was unaware Emerald had come to an abrupt stop and he nearly ran her over.

"Oh no, I'm sorry. Guess I wasn't paying attention."

"No harm done" she spoke, straightening her attire. She pointed to a tall tree standing in their way and with a flourish of her hand announced, "This is our *Tree Castle*. What do you think?"

Jamie's fingers were doing a drum roll on the sides of his trousers while he contemplated an answer. "Nice tree, I guess. Big. Green. I don't understand the castle part."

"Follow me. You'll be impressed." Circling around a small pond, the wind had turned the once quiet surface of it into a frenzy, blasting them with icy water. Quickly brushing through ferns and ivy, they reached the base of the huge tree, both of them now soaked to the bone. Emerald pushed her fingers into a recess of the tree and pulled open a hidden door. Jamie had to think a moment. The door seemed to be a normal size until he remembered he was now six inches tall and he could easily reach the top of the door frame. Stepping inside out of the weather, he found them in a large anteroom. The walls gave off a soft blue light that shown through Emerald's translucent wings, delicate as those of a butterfly. The light enhanced more than her wings though. She was like a painting from a master's brush put forth to gaze upon. *Wow*! Ebony black hair, emerald green eyes, silver slippers laced with silk, winding around her pretty legs in ribbons to tie above her calves, caused Jamie to stare like a puppet who could do nothing else.

"Jamie . . . You're staring at me."

"Oh, I'm sorry. This is all so overwhelming . . . You, the night . . . I'm still having difficulty reasoning what my eyes are showing me."

Emerald twirled a lock of her hair around her finger while she thought about Jamie's answer. He was really quite cute now that he was normal. Well, normal to her, now. His eyes though, did tell of the anxiety racing inside of him like a honeybee looking for pollen.

"I would probably feel the same way if I was whisked away into a different realm that I didn't even know existed. Jamie, I would not hurt you. My only mission was to save you from harm. Know that. Tomorrow you must return to your family, but for now, I want to show you our world."

Jamie took a deep breath, breathing out to expel the tension inside him. It worked. He did want to know more about this fairy who was stealing his heart away. He'd not had this much conversation with Shawn Leslie during the entire school year. Not with any girl for that matter. Well, except his sister Amy and that really didn't count. Why did he feel so at ease now with Emerald? *It didn't matter; just accept it* an inner voice lectured. "I don't think I even thanked you for doing what you did. Thank you. Two words are hardly compensation for what you've done for me."

"Given the chance, you would do the same for me. I know that. That is my compensation. You're wondering about the blue light, I can tell. The walls are painted with a compound made from plants and silt found in stream beds that retain energy from the sun." Emerald pointed to the ceiling above the door. "See that glass prism above you? They are placed on every floor allowing sun to shine through and re-energize the walls. The top of the tree is open as it was once hit by lightning. The tree smoldered inside for many years making it easy for the elves to remove the ashes and turn it into    their castle."

Jamie was impressed. The room was finished like a castle far and away more exquisite than his father's log cabin. The floors were marble, bouncing the blue light off the polished surface like a mirror. A stairway with steps carved into the tree circled the room to reach the ceiling and the next floor, guarded by an ornate, varnished banister. Emerald took hold of Jamie's hand and her touch took away any doubt about where he wanted to be right now. Never before had a touch swept him off his feet and into a warm fuzzy place where he never wanted to leave.

"Come meet my family and friends, you'll like them, and we    have a lot to talk about. It's been an amazing night so far, don't    you think?"

"I hope the rest of the night is not quite so amazing," Jamie answered, rolling his eyes.

As he spoke, the prism high above their heads in the ceiling flashed an intense blinding light in concert with a loud "boom." Jamie grabbed the banister for balance as the tree jolted like it was the epicenter of a large earthquake. They stood and stared at each other for a moment; the air around them, now still as death.

"That was very close" Jamie gasped, breaking the silence. I think that was lightening and the distance away where the lightening will touch down is measured by the gap of time between the flash and the thunder. There was none."

Wisps of blue smoke filtered down from the floor above through the opening where the stairway reached up to, carrying with it the scent of burning wood. Without a word, Emerald started up the spiral stairway with Jamie close behind. The next level was a storeroom for tools and goods. Overhead, the prism now flashed a reddish gold in a random pattern; smoke drifting down from the ceiling far above. Emerald picked up the pace, hurrying to the next level and the main living area. Coming through the passageway into the *Grand Hall*, smoke hovered below the high ceiling. The prism above was glowing brighter than the red lights on an ambulance. Elves and fairies alike scurried up the stairway above. An elf on the stairway caught sight of Emerald and hurried back to meet her.

"Emerald, we were worried. Thank God we've found you. I didn't know where you were. Mika has a plan to put the fire out, but we need to hurry before it gets ahead of us." Raal gave Jamie a quick look through piercing dark eyes, but there was no time now to devote more than a glance to the issue.  With a swish of his head sending long black hair away from his eyes in a flurry, he herded Jamie and Emerald toward the stairway.  Once inside the kitchen level, Jamie could see how the fire started.  The small round openings, or portals, that were spaced around the perimeter of the large room were at floor level.  The lightening must have hit the tree point blank.  Fire blasted through the tiny openings with extreme pressure, for the floor was scorched in lines in front of the portals reaching to the far end of the room.  Flames were now reaching up the castle walls with vicious intensity.

Emerald could see Cyra's form through the smoke, col- lapsed over a large kitchen table.  She knew what needed to be done.  She reached for the flute, the touch sending the power coursing through her veins as she ran toward her friend.  "Bring her over to a portal away from the fire, Mika," Emerald shouted reaching for a Valla Laun seed in her pouch.  Once in the end of the flute she aimed it toward the opening and blew.  The silver cord shot through the portal and coiled on the ground far below.  Reaching for the end of the cord coming from the flute, she swirled it around one of the heavy legs of the kitchen table and it melted together with itself.

"Raal, you're the strongest.  Take Cyra down the cord to somewhere near the pond.  The fresh air will revive her."

A young fairy with golden red hair falling to her waist in ringlets, walked with Cyra while Raal carried her toward the portal, her green eyes showing grave concern for her friend.

"Luna, you follow them down and watch over Cyra.  I don't want to leave her alone in her condition."

"Thank you, Emerald, I want to stay with her."

"Hurry back, Raal. I'm sure we will need your strength soon," Emerald said, watching them to make sure they reached the ground safely As soon as Luna was safe on the forest floor, everyone headed toward the stairway on their way toward the top level of the castle and the water room. Smoke poured through two of the portals where fire was trying to consume the outside of the castle. With a gust of wind, flames shot through the small openings like a blast from a dragon's mouth, nearly enveloping an elf named Bolo, the last up the stairs. He patted the smoke from his scorched blouse and hurried after the others. He was very frightened, Jamie could tell as the whites of his eyes were clearly visible surrounding green pupils, darting back and forth at the mayhem. Red scraggly hair shot out from under his cap in uncontrollable directions as he caught up with Jamie. Emerald hoped Mika had a very good scheme to end the disaster, otherwise they were surly going in the wrong direction. At the top of the stairway, she pushed open the trap door and was assaulted by a howling gust of wind. She held the door back for Bolo and three others as Raal raced up the stairway after them. The top of the hollow Tree Castle was open and exposed to the elements, but for now, the rain had passed leaving only the harsh wind.

Mika scratched the patch of furry white hair above his ear and exclaimed, "Just when we could use the rain, it decides to quit. Whose side are the clouds on anyway?"

"That's why they're called *dark clouds* Mika," yelled Raal, as he dropped the trap door back in place.

In the center of the massive room, loomed a large wooden barrel, the stays held in place by wide metal straps. The prisms were then set in the floor around the perimeter to catch the light. A wooden ladder, doweled to the side of the water barrel, led to the very top, making it possible to check the water level and to a catwalk. This led to a walkway around the top perimeter of the *Tree Castle* and acted as a lookout. Mika stood in front of the barrel. He seemed solemn as a preacher presiding at a funeral as he pushed his round spectacles up the bridge of his nose. A calloused hand wrapped around a long steel rod and a heavy sledge stood on the floor next to his feet. Smoke and fire billowed through the small perimeter portals at floor level, as he cleared his throat to speak.

"I've been up the ladder and the water barrel is full. Emerald make sure the handle on the trap door is turned to seal it tight. We're going to unleash a torrent of water. It's going to gush out the portals and put out the fire, guaranteed. That's if we can break the water loose. I'll hold this bar above one of the metal hoops and Raal; you take the sledge and pound it in between the hoop and two staves. After that is done, everybody grab hold and we'll break the staves out. When that happens, run for the ladder for the water is going to rise up fast. Let's get started. We can repair the barrel but not the whole tree and for sure, not our lives."

Raal beat the bar in between the staves with about five good swings and water hissed out around it soaking them all as they grabbed on to pull.

"On three everyone," Mika screamed. "One . . . Two . . . *Threeeee!"*

They all pulled with all their might, while water sprayed out at them from around the rod, but the staves would not break.

"Pickles," Mika cursed. "I was sure this would work. You gotta put your heart into it guys, so once more with feeling. Hey . . . Where's Bolo?"

Bolo was completely transfixed by the flames shooting through the portals with each gust of wind, unaware of the others.

"Bolo! Get over here. Darn him anyway. He's as strong as ten elves, but with the brain of a sow bug."

Emerald took the time to take a seed from her pouch. She let Bolo grab the bar in front of her and stuffed the seed into his back pocket. She took out her flute as Mika screamed.

"One . . . Two" ----

On *"three,"* she touched the flute to Bolo's back pocket. A blinding white light enveloped them all as three wooden staves broke loose in an instant. A torrent of water swished them all out across the floor like leaves in the wind.

"That worked," Mika wheezed, wiping the water from his eyes as he struggled to stand. "I keep forgetting you have all this dazzling power like Cyra had. Thanks, you saved the day."

"You're welcome. We're still fighting an up-hill battle, but we'll surely win," remarked, Emerald, wading through the fast-rising water"

"Wow!," Bolo exclaimed, batting his head with the palm of his hand. "What a feeling came over me. *Awesome!*"

Quickly they all sloshed toward the ladder and hopefully safety. The water was rising at an alarming rate now, for the portals were too small to handle so much so fast. Was it fear or the sudden rush of Emerald's magic that propelled a crazed Bolo toward the ladder in haste? He scooted up the rungs of the ladder like a squirrel scampering up a branch, not once looking back.

Jamie was standing on one of the rungs of the ladder about half-way to the top. He could see everyone was accounted for, except for a frail elf called Woon. Jamie turned and watched him struggle below against the raging current in vain. He was waist deep now in water, and the current kept pushing him sideways. He could read the fear in his eyes as he grabbed for the bottom rung of the ladder with his last surge of strength. The rung broke with a *pop,* and Woon was swept away like a twig in a stream still holding to the splintered piece of wood. He gasped for air, struggling to keep his head above the surface, choking and spitting out the cold water before he was forced to consume even more. Around the barrel he whizzed, three times now and getting closer to the whirlpools developing above the portals. It was easy enough for Jamie to see he would be sucked down and out one of the portals in no time at all, to fall and crash onto the forest floor far below. Without a thought for his own safety, Jamie jumped into the water just before Woon on his next time around the barrel. A strong swimmer in school, he felt confident he could save Woon's life. With his arm around Woon's chest, he paddled and kicked toward the barrel, but the current was proving to be too much for him. The added pull of the whirlpool was sucking them both down into a dark tunnel and surely oblivion. The fear he felt aboard the *Northern Bear* returned in an instant as he struggled to keep Woon's head above water. Then, from the corner of his eye, he caught sight of Emerald holding the silver flute and relief swelled in his heart. Why would he not know that she would save him? This was no time to reason why, but he knew he was surely blessed. She held her arm in the air and pointed at him with the flute. He understood. With one hand free, he kicked his feet like mad to stay afloat and held his arm in the air for he knew what was coming next. The silver cord shot from the flute, the end molding around his wrist only seconds before they would have been sucked below the raging torrent and shot out the portal to become part of history. A very long drop it would have been. The thought was terrifying, but there was not time to dwell on it. Now he could feel the sharp tug against his arm as Raal pulled them both out of a sure disaster and over to the ladder. Jamie pushed Woon against the barrel so Raal could grab him and sling him over his shoulder. Jamie climbed the rungs behind Raal who was carrying Woon and they made their way toward the catwalk high above.

***

Standing on the lookout walkway, they all peered out over the edge of the castle wall. The castle looked like a giant sprinkler as water shot out the portals in unison. The top of the portals was designed with a cleat that deflected some of the water downward to soak the tree trunk and all the close branches set ablaze by the lightning strike. It was working. Now there was not a flame left anywhere. Just smoke. Lots of it. If some of the nearby trees had caught fire, there was no sign of it now. Raal laid Woon down on the wooden walkway. He was still gasping for air and spitting out water, but alive, thanks to Emerald's friend. *Where did he come from?,* Raal wondered. "You probably won't care to ever see water again, Woon, but at least you'll be alive to make that decision thanks to whoever that was," Raal offered. Woon tried to focus his eyes on the voice coming from above but having little success in doing so. Raal knew that Woon most likely had no recollection of the last part of his swim in the water room, but he could see that his words were helping to revive him. Still looking dazed after his ordeal, Raal left him to recover, walking over to Jamie to pat him on the back. "Don't know where you came from or who you are, but you're definitely going to be a hero to Woon. That was a foolish act of bravery for which we are most grateful."

"Emerald just saved me from a similar circumstance from which I also would have perished, so I am glad to have a part of helping someone else."

Emerald took Jamie's hand.

"This is Jamie, Raal. I found him on a river boat broken loose in the storm. It was just hours ago and zapped him small so he could spend the night with us. Now look what happened? . . . *More disaster*, Emerald sighed. You were great though, Jamie. Few would be so brave."

"Few would have a chance like that to find out if they could be."

While they were talking, Woon pushed himself upright and wobbled toward them looking as pale as beach sand.

"What's going on? What happened to me? Is the forest on fire?"

Mika was the first to speak.

"You missed all the fun Woon, when you went for that swim. The fire is out, and we all survived. I can't say much for our Tree Castle though."

"It's fixable," remarked Gree, the youngest of the elves. "We need to celebrate."

"Celebrate . . . Celebrate? Celebrate what? Celebrate that our water system is broken, our castle is drenched and smells like a      fire pit?"

The crowd's response was immediate.

*Our castle still stands, we have won; ha -ha*

*The water has snuffed out the flames; tra-la*

*We all pulled together to save our fine home*
*And we weathered the crises quite well; ta-da*


*We thought we lost Woon, for he gave us a scare*
*Cyra looked frightful 'till she breathed in fresh air*
*The fire is out, but the scent isn't roses*
*The smoky disaster still burns in our noses*
*So we'll wash and we'll scrub, we'll polish and clean*
*'Till the castle looks fresh as we've ever seen*


*The bark has been charred to almost a powder*
*Leaves blackened and curled like a witch's dark curse*
*Ashes and soot mask the floors and the walls*
*Though it's made it through times we believe even worse*


*The water barrel's broken, the ladder is too*
*Glass prisms so smoky no light will shine through*
*So tomorrow we'll work from the top to the ground*
*But, what's really important, we're all safe and sound.*

*Our castle still stands, we have won; ha-ha*

*The water has snuffed out the flames; tra-la*

*We all pulled together to save our fine home*

*And we weathered the crisis quite well; ta-da*


*We've all survived lightning's perilous fire*

*And now it is safe, we can say*

*We can laugh, we can shout*

*We can dance, we can sing*

*With joy toward tomorrow's day*

\*\*\*

Joyous with the survival of their castle and possibly the survival of the whole forest, the elves screamed and hugged each other, bringing Jamie into the fold. Even Mika was emotional, which was quite unusual for one always so serious and stoic.

Woon was in a world of his own though, still suffering from emotional distress. He wobbled along the lookout walk alone, far away from the others, still coughing up water. Finally, he had to grab hold of the wall railing overlooking the pond for balance. It took a while for his brain to focus on what his eyes perceived far below. His head felt like the inside was filled with something like the dust particles that would dance in a ray of sun shining through the trees. What he finally saw though, when his brain and eyes finally connected, made his hair stand on end. A clan of pixies surrounding Cyra and Luna, were throwing stones at them, taken from pouches on their waist belts. Luna hovered over Cyra, shielding her from the blows, but Woon could see she was in dire trouble even though the distance from the top of the *Tree Castle* to the forest floor was extreme. Fear, anger and anxiety coursed through his veins like a comet, bringing him back to life in an instant.

"Emerald, Emerald, come quickly," he screamed in hoarse response to the ongoing crime. Emerald was there in a moment to look over the railing and could hardly believe what she saw. The forest floor looked like a war zone in progress and in utter chaos. Trails of smoke rose from burnt branches and charred bark washed from the once flaming trees, but that was only half of the desolation. Aghast, she could not believe pixies could be so despicable. True, they were definitely pranksters, usually after drinking mushroom tea, but this was a more serious event. The leader was Nanod, and Emerald knew him well. He was the bully of the clan. He was capable of goading others to do bad things they would not conceive of on their own; a terrible trait for one in charge of an entire clan. All pixies wore the same attire consisting of a forest green suit with red pointed shoes and cap with a round gold ornament sewn on top. Nanod though, stood out from the rest. He was overweight and sloppily dressed, which was unusual for a pixie. Red hair spiked out from under his cap like an unattended lawn and a devilish smirk never seemed to leave his lips. Now Emerald and Woon could hear the pixies chanting in unison.

# EMERALD

*Fairies, fairies can't you fly?*

*The reason leaves us unaware*

*We'll throw these stones, so you will try*

*So, show us if you dare.*


*It is hostility that we feel*

*Your perfection makes us mad*

*Why can't you be like us, you know?*

*Why can't you once be bad?*


*Fairies care, they love and nurse*

*With such goodness they're inclined*

*But goodness really makes us sick*

*And why are they so refined?*


*We have never seen a fairy*

*Who has let her figure go*

*Their hair is always clean and brushed*

*With ribbons to look just so*

*The scent of roses fills the air*

*If one just happens by*

*Their skin is soft and smooth as silk*

*Teeth white as milk and why?*


*Never has a fairy's wings*

*Or dress been soiled or creased*

*Extreme cleanliness for personal things*

*Is most fanatical to say the least*


*Fairies, fairies can't you fly*

*Oh fairies pure and fair?*

*We'll throw these stones to help you try*

*Please show us if you dare*


Turning on one of his own, Nanod hurled a stone at Trinket, the smallest of the clan, for not entering into the festivities. The stone hit him square above the eyes and he reeled in a circle trying to stay conscious.

"You're a wimp Trinket, so get out of here," he touted.

"We don't need your kind to just stand and gawk, so go home and hold on to your mommy's apron."

Trinket ran in a staggering, unbalanced line into the forest alone as Nanod turned again toward his victims. Luna's back was covered with welts and a trickle of blood appeared on her forehead. Consciousness might soon slip away and the worry that she then could not protect Cyra, forced her to hang on with all her might.

Emerald felt helpless. Helpless until she remembered her gift from Mother Nature. She grabbed the magic flute pulling it from the scabbard. With that small act of wrapping her fingers around the silver magical instrument, confidence again roared through her body like a storm.

"Hoooowaaaaah!", rang through the silence like thunder.

Jamie turned toward Emerald in wonder. How could so much sound come from such a dainty little fairy? Nanod and the rest of the pixies turned from their mission of violence to locate the owner of the war cry but failed. In the meantime, Emerald loaded a Valla Laun seed into the end of her flute and aimed directly at Nanod's. head. "Fizzzzzz." Nanod was enveloped in a ball of white light blazing the night sky brighter than a football field full of floodlights. Everyone had to cover their eyes with their hands and stare through their fingers. In only a few seconds the light was gone, but Nanod's clothes were left in tatters like the remnants of a flag after battle. Discouraged for only a moment, he looked around trying to find a reason for such an odd disaster. Then he saw her. Moonlight reflected off the silver flute, just as another Valla Laun seed expelled from its chamber.

*"Fizzzzzz."* There was no time to get out of the way. The moment was instant. Again, he was enveloped in a ball of white light. Inside the ball, the sound was intense.

*"Whrrrrhhhh."*

Nanod was left completely nude except for his red pointed shoes and hair that looked like hay blowing in the wind. He tried to stand upright, but what a task. He recognized the symptoms. The feeling was the same as spinning in circles for fun then trying to walk a straight line. The rest of the clan had scattered, leaving him without clothing or esteem. Embarrassed beyond belief, Nanod covered his private parts with his hands and stumbled quietly in a squiggly line into the darkness, leaving Cyra and Luna hurt and alone, but safe for now.

"Follow me when you can," yelled Emerald as she jumped from the *Tree Castle* to reach her friends on the ground.

"I really don't care to jump from this height to become mulch," was Mika's response, coming from under his breath.

"Of what service to others would I be then? The water room will soon be empty, and we can take the stairs," he muttered, straightening his spectacles then gathering the others.

"I'm sure that's what she had in mind anyway," replied Raal. "Whizzo, what a night this has been."

Mika pushed his spectacles up the bridge of his nose again and turned to Jamie.

"Your home is going to seem rather boring to you, or should I say restful, after participating in all these strange events, don't you think?"

"I haven't had time to think about it, for everything happens so fast around here it seems. But yes, I guess my life was comparably dull, although at the time I wasn't aware of it."

# Chapter Eight

Back safe in the Grand Hall of the *Tree Castle*, blue light still emanated from the painted walls, even though fine soot seemed to have settled on every inch of the floor, tables and chairs. The elves and Jamie worked vigorously to clean the worst of it up, while Emerald attended to Luna's cuts and bruises. Bolo brought down spiced cider in pitchers, and hot biscuits with honey from the kitchen, setting it all on the table. Making another trip up the stairs, he brought back silver goblets, lighting several candles that gave a warm, flickering glow to the Grand Hall. Jamie, for now had nearly forgotten about his other family and his eyes wandered around the unbelievable Grand Hall. Really, his parents' log cabin seemed so crude in comparison. Stairways with polished wood banisters wound upward around the perimeter of the huge hall, high into the next level, almost disappearing from sight. The walls gave off a pale blue glow that mirrored on the glass prism centered on the gleaming marble floor. A gold railing glistened around the prism, all of which was breathtaking. It must have taken forever to accomplish such a feat, he thought, especially considering the small size of the clan. But what really caused a fuzzy warm feeling in the center of his heart was Emerald. It was hard to take his eyes off of her as she nursed Luna's wounds.

From the corner of her eye, Emerald could feel she was being watched and she blushed, the tips of her pointed ears turning pink. She could easily sense Jamie had a crush on her and it warmed her heart. But there was a certain sadness in that realization. They were from different realms and soon must part. *Oh pickles!*

"I'm sure your parents are worried about you Jamie. Do they know where you are?" Emerald began as she turned toward her friend.

Emerald's words brought Jamie back to a reality he had pushed far into the recesses of his mind. *His family.* Now, worry began seeping into his heart like fog around a mountain. He pictured his mother wringing her hands as she sat on the hearth wondering if she would ever see her boy again. Guilt was at the forefront of his thoughts, and the reason was simple. He was not even trying to get back home and relieve his mother's pain. But in answering Emerald's question, emotions surfaced that he could not control, and he wiped tears from his cheek with the pad of his finger. *What could you do now on your own anyway* his mind reminded him? *You're no larger than a blade of grass. Emerald will help you find your parents.* With those thoughts in mind, Jamie was able to relax somewhat, and he cleared his throat.

"I did some stupid things, I must admit. I went into the forest to hunt with an air rifle, which was against my mother's advice. Because of that, I did not tell anyone what I was about to do. They have no idea what happened to me. I'm sure of that. Darkness crept up on me and then the storm came. It is a miracle that I'm still alive. Actually, I wouldn't be if not for you."

Emerald left Luna to hug her friend in a long embrace and her heart swelled in the closeness of their touch. "Trust in me, Jamie; you'll be fine."

"I do Emerald, I do trust you", he whispered.

By now, everyone had found a seat around the huge table, and were sampling the hot biscuits and cider. Jamie continued talking about his sister, parents, and school. All, which seemed so ordinary and boring, next to their fantastic lives. For some reason though, they found his stories most interesting, just as their experiences were to him. He was caught up in the comradeship and love they shared in a realm he never knew existed. *Wow!* Above all, Emerald was so beautiful in poise and behavior; he was being drawn to her by a force he never before experienced in his thirteen years. He'd always felt insecure around girls but with Emerald, that was not the case. He felt perfectly at ease in her company, as they ate, drank, sang and told stories far into the night.

Emerald watched Jamie from across the table. She was becoming attached to him more than she should, she began to realize. She was responsible for his welfare, and that's what a Fairy Princess should do. But it was important not to upset the order of the universe by the use of magic. That was one of Mother Nature's most solemn rules. Her job was to return him to his family at first light in his normal condition. Feelings of the heart must not interfere with what she knew was just and right. She brushed a tear from her eye with the pad of her finger as she stood and raised her hand. A hush fell over the *Grand Hall.*

"As you all know by now, Jamie is a human I magically made small, so he could stay safe with us until we could return him to his family at first light."

"Hasn't been that safe Emerald", Mika offered, pushing his spectacles up the bridge of his nose.

"Although I might add," he went on, "you did the noble thing, and I'm sure he's better off here than alone and out in the storm."

"Thank you, Mika," Emerald offered. Emerald's green eyes focused on Jamie and a warm sensation buzzed through his veins until he was sure he was floating on air.

"Jamie, you have been a true friend, one who has proved he would give his life for us. Woon can attest to that."

Sitting next to Jamie, Woon pulled him close with a hug. Embarrassed, Jamie's ears turned bright red from the gesture, but it was neat being a part of this unusual clan.

"But now we need to get you back to the river," Emerald continued. "Your parents need to find you safe and sound, for I'm sure they are worried sick over your disappearance."

Jamie couldn't help but feel sad, for this was the experience of his life and he bit into his lip as his mind pondered the reality that he might never see these people again. *Never see Emerald. Forever!* Emerald could see the sadness in his eyes and yes, the moment was having the same effect on her. Being a Princess was a thrill beyond belief, but this was the downside to the title. Emerald tapped her finger against her lips in thought as a plan formed in her mind to return Jamie. Everything must come together at first light with nothing left to chance. Funny how in charge she seemed to be, for this was not the Emerald she knew as herself. Sure, once the flute was in her touch, she had unbelievable powers, but something else was happening inside her. She was becoming more confident and her eyes sparkled with this new knowledge about herself.

"Mika would all of you go out and find Ma. She is so nosey, I'm sure she is close. She must find the wolves so they can lead Jamie's family to him. I would like a moment alone with Jamie and then we will meet you by the pond."

Jamie gasped, as the clan filed down the stairway.

"Wolves . . . Did you say *wolves?* "

A shudder ran through his body like the storm he just experienced.

"They are our friends, Jamie. They can find your family and guide them to the river where they will find you."

"Seems very scary to me to trust a wolf. *And you say wolves?* How many are there?"

"Three, a father, mother and son, and I would trust them with my life."

"If you say so, I surely trust your judgment, but it does go against everything I've been taught about wolves."

"Did you believe in fairies and elves?," Emerald asked, smiling across the table at him.

Jamie rolled his eyes as feelings of dismay floated around in his brain like dust in the wind. "At this point, I'm beginning to realize a lot of things I've been taught don't really hold water. I'm sure there are a lot more surprises waiting for me if I can only remember to question authority more."

Jamie's mind began scrolling through the night's events, with the realization that it might all too soon, come to a screeching halt. It had only been hours since he first met Emerald, but his world before that time seemed very distant for some reason. This night would forever now, change the way in which he would see himself and the world around him.

As the sound of the clan's footsteps disappeared down the stairway, Jamie got up from the table and walked over to Emerald, taking hold of her hand.

*This night I was alone in pain*

*I prayed for help and no one came*

*I felt despair, could life end here?*

*Did God not hear? My heart knew fear*

*Then . . .*

*I heard a voice, I turned to see*

*Such beauty standing close to me*

*Could you be real?*

*Could I not be sane?*

*Then a whisper from within*

*Said you prayed and someone came*

*Friends we'll always be, forever*

*No one can change that, no not ever*

*I know I must leave you*

*I don't want to go*

*When I leave I know*

*I will miss you so*


*Your skin was like cream so white*

*Enhanced by shafts of moon's warm light*

*Your cheeks and shoulders hinted blush*

*A portrait from a master's brush*


*I hope in time we meet again*

*That is my dream, my every wish*

*In a forest washed clean with rain*

*Long before a morning mist*


Emerald hugged Jamie, and they stayed quietly in that special closeness, as tears welled in her eyes. What a profound impact she evidently made on him and her heart swelled with that knowledge. Jamie had touched her the same way, but she had not allowed herself to listen to those inner voices and feelings. The rules of the forest were not to be upset for whatever reason. Emerald unhooked a silver necklace from around her neck and placed it in Jamie's pocket.

"You will wake on the riverbank at first light and your first thought will be, *was this all a dream?* This gift shall remind you that it was not."

With that Emerald kissed Jamie and it was the first time in her thirteen years she had ever felt warm lips against hers. A kiss that nearly matched the moment when she first touched the magic flute and she felt her legs go all wobbly. She could tell Jamie had the same experience. She stood back and grinned.

*Your heart is a locket, it will hold the emotions*

*And feelings we've shared this night*

*A vision, a touch, a sound, a scent*

*Kept safe from the world's skeptic light*


*The key to your locket is my name my friend*

*To open and let treasures free*

*To remember and feel our love once again*

*In this night we have shared you will see*

*You broke through the veil that conceals our realm*

*From your soul you cried out a prayer*

*I ran through the night toward emotions I felt*

*My body could feel your despair*


*You are my friend, I love you*

*I shall hold this night in my heart*

*My friend, alas, I'll miss you*

*All too soon before dawn, we must part.*


*If ever peril's shadow falls heavy again*

*Please will you call out my name?*

*I will rush to your side in a moment*

*Your prayer will not be in vain*


Hand in hand, Emerald and Jamie walked down the wide circular stairs carved into the perimeter of the Tree Castle's trunk and out the secret door leading to the pond. Looming next to the fairies and elves was Ma. To Jamie, she looked like a giant feathered airplane, forgetting for a moment how very small he was now. She straightened her tilted spectacles with the tip of her wing, and focused on Jamie, like he was a specimen in a jar in the school science room. She turned her neck in almost a full circle and the bones cracked as she leveled her yellow-gold eyes directly at him. His heart skipped a beat.

"Phooey on arthritis. It's going to be the death of me," she spoke in perfect English, patting down a kerchief around her neck.

Jamie relaxed as Ma's gaze looked away from him to focus on Emerald. Funny, but a talking owl now seemed quite natural in the scope of events that was throwing darts at his sanity.

"Emerald, I'll get your message to the wolves," Ma began. "No problem. Getting humans to follow wolves could be an issue. Those two species are not the best of friends you know?"

"Wally is ingenious. He will find a way. Trust me, it will work."

Ma clucked her tongue, shaking her head.

"You're the Princess, what do I know? I hope for your sake it all works out. As you know, I'll have no trouble in locating them. Knowing where everyone is has become an obsession with me."

"I know Ma, *I know*."

Effortlessly, Ma flew into the night sky, and banked sideways through the trees without as much as a breath of sound. One of her feathers floated next to Jamie, its length taller than he. He exhaled in disbelief. At that moment, Emerald laid her hand on Jamie's shoulder and whispered, "Don't worry Jamie; the wolves will make this work for us. Ma is way too cynical. It is in her nature to be that way. Come, we should be on our way. We have quite a distance to go."

# Chapter Nine

The storm had passed, but the forest floor was wet and cluttered with debris from its violent passage making Emerald's journey with Jamie and her clan difficult. But nevertheless, spirits were high as they marched through the darkness with a spring in their step. Hey, the whole night had been a test of perseverance and none of them were going to be pressed down by a little inconvenience. In single file, they pushed through the thick brush and tall trees with only the light of the full moon piercing through the green canopy where it could find an occasional opening. Cyra was in the lead. The crisp night air had done wonders for her, and she now felt strong as ever.

Quite some time had passed when Cyra came to an abrupt stop signaling everyone to be still. She strained forward and listened, a hand cupped in back of her pointed ear. There was only a whisper through the trees, but in the stillness after the storm, the words were definite.

*"Help me . . . Someone please help me."*

Emerald heard the voice also and steeled past Cyra through the trees. There, against a tall tree, the smallest pixie, Trinket, sat holding his leg, obviously in great pain. A huge bump swelled above his eyebrow from the stone thrown by Nanod. But something else was going on before Emerald's eyes that skipped her attention at first glance. She began to notice the extreme fear in Trinket's eyes as he stared out into the darkness. That wasn't the look of pain. No way. Instantly Emerald gasped as she was made aware of the real problem. A massive black snake stared down at Trinket, his lengthy body coiled beneath him. "Rep" was out of sorts. A bully by nature on the best of days, the Rain Forest was proving to be not a good place for him. He needed warmth from the sun against his skin to exist, which wasn't going to happen under all these trees and pounding rain. Escaping from a delivery truck, where he was held hostage inside a barrel of oats, was proving to be the mistake of his life when he realized what the climate here was really like. He needed a warm rock to sun himself on or wind up in snake heaven, wherever the heck that was. Anyway, he was sure hungry. Anxiety made him hungry. Stress made him hungry. The wet and cold made him hungry. Everything made him hungry. All in all, Rep was just plain miserable and hungry. Actually, misery was his constant companion, and now poor Trinket was going to pay the price of Rep's deprived existence with his life.

*Ah-ha! I've found a victim*

*Although he's kind of small*

*Oh well, it's better to 'ave had hors d'oeuvres*

*Than not to 'ave dined at all*


*I'm a snake a-wake, a repi-tile*

*I slither in the night*

*Harassing those who cross my path*

*I really cause them fright. Hah!*

*I don't need arms and legs or hands and feet*

*'cause that would slow me down*

*Extremities aerodynamically are known to be unsound*

*I must find a victim every night*

*I can't help it, its compulsion*

*To torture and maim, to bully and scare*

*Is a psychological addiction*

*Why am I so darn angry?*

*Is therapy what I need?*

*Were genes from mom and dad all bad?*

*Was I a dysfunctional seed?*

*It is said my body smells*

*But, if it does, I don't take notice*

*I'm not in tune with personal hygiene*

*That's something I care not to practice, 'cause*

*My tail starts behind my eyes*

*Leaving nothing in between uh huh*

*For hands and feet or paws and claws*

*To help me scour and clean*


*My eye will twitch, my mouth gets dry*
*My nerves will sing and whine*
*But when there's one to dominate*
*My mind and body's fine*


*A year I'll go without a meal*
*And a pound I'll hardly lose*
*But a night without some violence*
*Is something I'd never choose*


*I hate, I hate*
*I want to cause some pain ah ah*
*I really love to hate you know?*
*I guess I am insane*


*I like to hiss and lunge and bite*
*How did I get so mean? ah ah*
*I wanna' corner someone; cause them fright*
*I wanna' feel them screeeeeem!*

Emerald edged closer until she was in Trinket's sight, taking the magic flute from the scabbard. Again, the energy flooded her body in an unbelievable rush, but she remained calm knowing what to expect now. She took a Valla Laun seed from her pouch, being mindful not to distract Rep, for at this point, he was unaware he was being watched.

"Trinket, we will get you out of this. Are you hurt?"

Trinket did not answer. He could not take his eyes off of Rep as though he was hypnotized.

"Snakes do not have ears. He cannot hear you," Emerald called out. "Are you hurt?"

"I think my leg is broken; I cannot move it. He's going to eat me, Emerald, I know it." Tears welled up in Trinket's eyes, his mouth scrunched to one side as he bit into his lower lip.

"We'll see about that."

Emerald blew a seed toward the ground away from Trinket using the flute like a pea shooter. There was a ball of white light and Rep struck at it. Before he could recover, another seed found its mark between his eyes and exploded. The blinding flash lit up the forest for a moment. Rep reeled back and forth like a stock of corn in the wind. He had forgotten about Trinket now and was trying to deal with this new problem. His left eye began to twitch. *Not a good sign.*

With another seed leaving the flute and causing the blast of light on the forest floor, Rep struck out again. Jamie took a step back, bumping into Bolo who was running the palms of his hands over his forehead in anguish, mumbling incoherently. Jamie could understand his plight easy enough. *Gee whiz*, he was frizzed too. Snakes were scary enough in the zoo behind thick glass, but this was taking terror to a whole new level. Being so small made Rep seem more like a medieval dragon than a snake, and with the ability to consume them all without a thought, and without leaving a trace. As Rep's face shot forward with his jaws spread wide apart, a fine mist trailed from the corners of his mouth sparkling in the moonlight. The clan *shuddered* at the sight. The snake's skin wrinkled and flexed under the effort, and the smell? *Stifling!* No wonder he was alone. His scent matched his hideously threatening demeanor, which could only be described as repulsive. Jamie noticed that Emerald, Mika and Raal seemed to remain quite calm as if this was an everyday experience. How these beings so small could have so much confidence was amazing.

A plan was forming in Emerald's mind. She turned from Rep and blowing into the flute shot the silver cord through the night sky toward the river, now only the length of a football field away. The cord swung over a heavy branch of a tree that hung over the fast-moving water, the end coiling to the ground on the bank. She pulled the other end from the flute wrapping a turn around her waist belt. "Raal, hurry and retrieve the end of the silver cord. We're going to wrestle this reptile down to the water and see if he can swim."

That moment proved dangerous, as Rep had time to focus on the flute. *That was where the ball of light was coming from,* his small little brain shouted from inside his head. He struck once again, and with his teeth, ripped the silver flute away from Emerald's fingers. Jamie's heart was in his throat watching Rep draw back with a smirk on his lips, the flute sticking out of the corner of his mouth like a glass thermometer. Emerald though, was not fazed by the small glitch in her plan. She calmly waited for Raal to deliver the end of the silver cord as she took another Valla Laun seed from her pouch. "Jamie, you and the others hang on to that cord and pull like you've never pulled before after I wrap the other end around Rep's tail right behind his eyes. We'll slide him over the forest floor and up the tree. He's going to put up a fight, but he can't get at us as long as we pull harder than he does. Rep was now in control . . . *He thought.* Being a bully, it was important to own the moment. He lowered his head to stare directly into Emerald's face, and only inches away, his evil black eyes staring, opaque as polished stone. Sometimes confidence can lead to an act of foolishness, if one is not fully prepared for what may follow. It was fairly easy now for Emerald to place a Valla Laun seed in Rep's nose. Truth be told, Rep should not have put his face that close to her. "*Whew,* she muttered," wrinkling her nose. Being that near to him, she had to brace herself from a blast of his hot breath and then the stench that followed. Jamie couldn't believe what she did. What courage. Just the thought of doing such an act made his knee's tremble. Emerald reached forward with lightning speed and grabbed the tip of the flute sticking out between Rep's teeth, and *whishhhh!* There wasn't much light this time at all as the blast happened internally when Rep breathed in the seed. His body turned transparent and swelled grotesquely for a moment leaving him completely out of sorts. A strange smoke and a hissing sound tore from Rep's nose sending Emerald's hair into disarray

Without a moment lost, Emerald took the cord from her waist belt and swung it around Rep's neck, and it melted together on itself. She jumped back behind Jamie and grabbed hold of the other end. It took a while for Rep's head to clear and to realize he was duped, but then his anger reached a new level. *The tug of war began.* "Pull," Emerald shouted as Rep took up the slack and they all dug their heels into the ground. Because the cord was pulling from the limb above the river, fairies, elves and Jamie were able to stay a safe distance from Rep, but it was still scary. The ground shook like they were struck by an earthquake as Rep thumped and flailed and flailed and thumped to get free, but so far to no avail.

Within minutes, was all it took for Emerald to realize they were not in control anymore. Rep had too much muscle and they were losing footing. At this rate they would soon find *themselves* in the river instead of Rep. If they let go of the cord, they would be chased down and devoured by a very angry snake. How could she have underestimated their ability? The outlook seemed grim, but then . . . It was only a glint of gold she saw out of the corner of her eye. Somewhere in the darkest trees, the full moon had given her the clue. It was the round ornament on a pixie's cap. They were *watching.* Now they needed to become performers. This was not just about saving Trinket. They were all at risk. Rep's tail was throwing plants, leaves, mulch and debris into the air as if a cyclone had touched down, as it whipped and banged across the forest floor making it difficult to see or even breathe. Only now there was a chance they could still win regardless of the sad way things were beginning to shape up.

"Nanod and all you pixies, I know you're out there watching," screamed Emerald, as she tugged on the silver cord, her heels still sliding through the mulch at even a faster rate.

"Rep is a menace to us all, not just Trinket. He needs to be stopped. With your help we can do it."

Still, there was no movement seen through the dark trees, but Emerald wasn't one to give up. *Ever*!

"Nanod . . . What are you afraid of? I thought you liked excitement. Or is it you can't even lead your clan to save one of your own?," Emerald screamed.

The dark forest remained quiet, but only for a few more moments. Emerald had hit an exposed nerve in Nanod's thick skull. At first there were only a few pixies coming forward, but with their bravery, the excitement was soon to spread. Pixies dwell on excitement, this Emerald knew for a fact. *Whoop's* filled the night air as the whole clan raced to join the tug of war. The power was now on Emerald's side and Rep found himself skidding along the ground at an alarming rate. He tried to wrap his tail around shrubs and branches to halt his decent toward the river, but that too, proved hopeless.

Rep could not hear, but if he could, he would have felt even more insecure. *Screams of "Eeeehaaaa, wheeeee, pull mates,"* filled the night's silence in the most rousing show of force imaginable. The comradeship was intense. *Insane!*

Back to where Trinket sat in pain, the voices faded in the distance until *his* forest was once again, still as death. He knew some of the voices were from his clan. He felt proud they would come to his rescue, but now fear entered the corners of his mind as the stillness consumed him. Had Rep won? He shuddered at the thought. What could he do now, unable to move with a broken leg? He could pray.

*Oh Mother Nature hear my prayer*

*We need your help so awfully bad*

*All my friends may perish soon*

*I find that very sad*


*My friends caused pain, I could not watch*

*I ran in shame, but for me they came*

*They stood with pride and faced their fear*

*If they're harmed, then I'm to blame*

*I feel his hot breath on my face*

*Soon I'll disappear without a trace*

*Is it darkness that summons fear?*

*And imagination that screams Rep is near?*


*I've never been this way, so helpless*

*Nor have I ever felt so small*

*But I'm proud my friends would fight for me*

*I saw them give their all*


*It's scary being all alone*

*In the dark*

*In the wet*

*In the cold*

*It's scary being all alone*

*When danger lurks so bold*


Back at the river's edge, amid the whoops and cries of the war party, Rep was tugged up the tree to the branch overlooking the dark, frothy river. Actually, he hung below the branch, suspended by the silver cord, his long black tail wagging downward in the moonlight like a piece of black rope in the wind.

"Keep pressure on the cord," Emerald announced, stepping out of line, reaching for her magic flute. Now, the forest was perfectly still as everyone looked up at Rep who seemed docile as a stuffed animal. The only movement was the twitch in his left eye as he stared back in silence at the throng of beings, holding fast to the silver cord. Instinctively he knew his fate was sealed. There was no option left and no hope of reprieve at this point. His coal black eyes stared down at the cold water and then over at Emerald walking toward him with that frightening shiny stick. Things were not looking good at all.

The clan looked on, as Emerald reached up and touched the cord with the tip of the flute. The cord *vanished* in the blink of an eye. Rep seemed suspended in mid-air for a moment, as if glued to some black tapestry. His eyes widened to twice their normal size, knowing the water would be freezing cold against his skin. Then without fanfare, as the two clans looked on, he fell into the fast-moving river and was swept away in an instant like a twig from a tree. At this point, everyone cheered and threw their pointed caps in the night air. Life was good.

Emerald was the first to speak.

"When Rep is finally able to get ashore, he will be far from here and in a warmer spot which would suit him just fine. I can't say we will miss his presence though. Not in the least."

A round of applause filled the night air and Emerald raised her arms, her outstretched fingers and palms facing her audience.

"Nanod, I must say that you carried your mischievousness to an unacceptable extreme earlier, but you came through tonight and saved us from extinction for which we are most grateful. Thank you Nanod, and thank you all."

Clapping and cheering once more prevailed, as Nanod beamed from ear to ear. Praise was a tribute that always went to another, so Emerald's words were like a special gift. In the meantime, more pixies appeared through the trees, now with shiny brass horns, drums, cymbals, and string instruments. Jamie could not believe what came next. It was dancing but appeared more like a tumbling act than anything he had ever witnessed, spurred on by a very strange chant sung by the chorus.

*Pee-foe-tee-moe Nah- nah-kah-mah La-ma-cu-lu-mow-mow*

*Loon–ah-mum-bah Did-em wahd-em Zoo- la-rule Ah-re-bah*

*Me-bah-lee-bah See-bah-koo-noo Bom-a-bam A-bim-bit*

*Kahm-a-dee-mee Wham-ah-ruz-ee Wall-a-wall A-whiz-oh*

*Oooooooohhhhh    Aaaaaaahhhhh*


*Mee-mee-dee-bee Oh-moe-toe-doe Nah-nah-la Ma-bo-boo*

*Tu-neu-tee-nee Did-en-wid-en Mud-en-bid En-clee-moe*

*Lee-bee-wee-bee- Fee-fil-kee-mah Wahm-bah-ma Moe-moe-ma*

*Nah-nah-la-la Na-na-la-la Tee-nee-tee Nah-tee-nee*

*Eeeeeeeeeeee    Aaaaaaahhhhh*


*Nah-nah-la-la Nah-nah-la-la Tee-nee-tee Nah-tee-nee*

*Nuz-ee-na-nuz Ee-na-raz-ah-la*

*Oooooooohhhhh    Aaaaaaahhhhh*

Jamie could not understand a word of it, but *wow,* if it didn't sound great as the chorus swayed back and forth, encouraging the dancers to outdo themselves.

# *Chapter Ten*

Nanod was artistically handicapped although not aware of it. He danced with the rest of them with just as much passion, but the result was comical. He just didn't have any rhythm in his bones, but no one really cared. Having fun was what Nanod was all about, when Emerald confronted him in haste.

"We need to get Trinket. He was hurt. *Remember?,"* Emerald remarked, tapping Nanod on the shoulder. *What is he thinking?,* she wondered.

"*Wow*, I completely forgot."

Nanod waved for silence and in moments the music and dance came to an awkward halt as everyone finished their individual step or note and looked to their leader.

"We need to get Trinket. Did you guys forget or something? *Let's go.*"

It took less time to get back to Trinket as they were not tugging on a snake's hostile efforts to get free from bondage, and was Trinket happy to see his clan again, unhurt.

"The forest was so still; I was scared the snake might have won. What happened?"

Emerald was the first to answer.

"He went for a swim in the river."

"He'll like it better downstream," Nanod offered.

"No" exclaimed Mika, "We'll like it better with him downstream."

Emerald kneeled beside Trinket taking the silver flute from its scabbard and laying it on the moss. Jamie hadn't noticed it before, but as the silver flute touched against her leg, the tips of her pointed ears showing through her ebony hair turned a light shade of pink and a flood of sparkles left her wings and dissipated into the night sky. The more he learned of her, the more fascinated he became. She ran her fingers over Trinkets leg with care, as he sat nervously awaiting the outcome. He squinted his eyes shut, and pressed his lips hard together, expecting severe pain to follow as Emerald's hand moved over the wound, but that did not happen.

"Hmm, you're in luck Trinket. The bone is still in place. We can make a splint from twigs and cloth and a stretcher from fern bows. You will need to stay off of it for a few weeks, but then you'll be as good as new."

"Thank you, Emerald. You had every right to look the other way after what we did to Cyra and Luna."

"First of all Trinket, *you* didn't throw any stones, *you* were hit by one just as Luna was. The proof is in that bump on your head. What your friends did was mean, but by being mean back to them only escalates the problem causing more anger. By coming together, like we just did, we rid the forest of evil and that is what Mother Nature expects of us. Not to fight and argue among ourselves."

Nanod sheepishly came up next to Emerald, trying to straighten his ill-fitting attire borrowed to cover up the few strips of material that were left after his encounter with the magical Valla Laun seeds.

"I'm sorry, Emerald. I hurt your friends. I don't know what gets into me at times, but I really feel bad about what happened this time. Now, I know one thing for sure though. I have a lot of respect for you and your family for what you did today. That was awesome what you did to the *Rep*. He picked on the wrong fairy." Emerald was quiet but pulled Nanod close, hugging him, the gesture speaking louder than words. Jamie was impressed. To have to leave these beings was going to be a hard moment to deal with but soon he must. *Darn.*

***

Three lights flashed randomly through the dense forest like fireflies looking for a place to land. It was Ken, Laura, and Amy Larson, all holding hands as not to get separated in the dark. Searching, searching, *searching*.

"Jamie . . . Jamie," the words interrupted the dark stillness as they listened for an answer from their son. *None came!*

"Oh Ken, Laura whispered, struggling with her emotions and on the brink of despair.

"I'm beginning to feel it's hopeless. We've been searching most the night. Our poor child, what could have happened?"

"I'm scared Mom – Dad," Amy began. "Could Jamie have been eaten, maybe mauled and dragged away or something?"

"Amy," Laura snapped. "Please don't say things like that. You cause my imagination to go nuts."

"I'm betting on Jamie," Ken soothed. "He's pretty knowledgeable about the forest. But come daylight, we'll definitely call in for more help. That will speed things up." With those words, Ken pushed some branches aside and became rigid as a lamp post.

"What's wrong" Laura whispered, looking around Ken's shoulder?

*"Oh no"* she gasped, her eyes not wanting to see what was before her. Her heart seemed to bump against her throat making further speech near impossible. With just enough moonlight to make them seem ghostlike, three wolves sat on their haunches, sniffing the air, their piercing golden eyes staring directly at the Larson's. Laura tugged on Ken's coat just as a blood curdling *"scream"* seared the stillness coming from Amy's mouth, open wide, and as round as a donut. Laura's hand cupped over Amy's lips, distorting her face somewhat, her shrieking voice reduced to unintelligible *mumbles*.

"Quiet," she ordered. Just then Willy Wolf spoke:

*The three people we've been tracking*

*I can see them now; oh wow!*

*They just saw me seeing them.*

*They are panicked now, and how*

*Listen to the small one scream*

*I've never heard that done*

*You see their mouths?*

*You see their eyes?*

*I think that they will run*


"Stand real still. Don't look scared," Ken warned, but Amy was beside herself. The next note from her lips was high pitched, with the vibrato of an opera star, sending a chill up Ken's spine. Laura pulled her close, clamping both hands over her face, so that only a *"hum"* pressed through her fingers.

"Wolves can tell when we're scared by the way we smell."

"Then they know I'm scared, Ken. That is something I can't hide."

Unlike his family, Ken didn't look upset. In a calm manner, he seemed to be analyzing the wolves' behavior, arms crossed over his chest in deep thought.

"I don't understand," he began, clearing his throat. "They should turn and run or attack, but they just sit there on their haunches and stare at us.  Most unusual.  The large wolf looks real familiar to me, Laura."

"What do you mean familiar?," Laura responded.  Ken could hear that her shaky voice was much higher than usual.  He turned to witness the fright in her eyes and squeezed her hand with affection.

"I mean I shot him with a dart once."

"Oh, great Ken," Laura wheezed.  "Who would need more of a reason for revenge?"

"It wasn't like that, dear.  I put him to sleep so I could get his paw out of a trap, sew up the wound and pour antiseptic on it."

Wally wolf thumped his tail on the forest floor, staring with curiosity at the three humans.

*The fairies said they lost their child*

*Through the forest they've searched this night*

*But we will guide them to their son*

*So they will find him at first light*

*The fairies said these three won't shoot*

*For some reason they are tame*

*But cautious we should surely be*

*And scatter if a gun they aim*

Wanda wolf nudged Wally, her eyes narrowing at his.

It seemed like a very bad mistake to her to put so much trust in humans.

*Humans act so very differently*

*Though by looks they seem the same*

*I hope these three aren't vicious*

*How do the fairies know they're tame?*


Wally shook his head, still thumping his tail.

*Well I know the tall one with short hair*

*He once was kind to me*

*He loosed me from a poacher's trap*

*Healed my paw and set me free*


Wanda glared at Wally, still not convinced yet by just a single act of kindness.

*But some set traps so they might catch us*

*Then maybe shoot us full of holes*

*Or maybe set out food to poison us*

*Then use our fur for clothes*

*They might stuff us like a Teddy Bear*

*On a wall they'll have us mounted*

*One of the trophies' shown their friends*

*They will brag of lives' they've ended*


*We cannot forage for our food*

*And live on berries, leaves and grass*

*We're designed to eat more protein*

*Which gives us strength instead of gas*


*But humans hunt just for the thrill*

*It's what they call a sport*

*They could not be too sensitive*

*If for that they'd kill or hurt*


*I'd say they're poor at tracking*

*I don't think that they can smell*

*If through this night they've searched and searched*

*Then they've really not done so well*


*I think humans must be low*

*On evolution's graded scale*

*Do you think they have a conscience?*

*If you could test them would they fail?*


*Humans, they shouldn't want to be*

*If a choice they had*

*Like us I think they'd wanna be*

*We lean on clever, not on bad*


Willy listened intently to his mother, but he began to see a side of his mother he hadn't noticed before. Her eyes were still narrowed on either his dad or the frightened humans below them.

*Mom, you're very negative*

*These three are scared, I know*

*They're worried sick about their son*

*They must miss him so*


*They must follow us, but how?*

*They don't speak our language, Dad.*

EMERALD

Wally had been working on a plan ever since Ma had
relayed Emerald's message to them.  Like everything in his
life, the parts of the puzzle just fell into place.  *What was
there to worry about?*


*Signs will be our language*

*They will understand my lad*


*With signs, you speak with actions*

*It's kind of like a game*

*A human saw me yawn once*

*And it made him do the same*


*Let your tongue hang down the side of your mouth*

*Then pant with a smile on your face*

*Don't bare you teeth or growl or bark*

*The fear that will cause will not erase*


*Wag your tail, That shows you're happy*

*Don't let your hair stand on end*

*I hope they'll feel we'll not attack*

*And want to be their friend*

107

*We'll fall back upon our haunches*

*And then we'll paw the air you see?*

*Then slowly turn around like this*

*And run two steps or three*


*We'll turn and face them once again*

*If they follow, we'll soon see*

*If they cannot grasp, we'll try again*

*They'll catch on most certainly*

Reluctantly, Wanda gave her approval by not saying anything. She could argue until she was blue in the face and still not change Wally's mind. Sometimes his cool disposition was maddening. If his plan went sour, as it seemed it very well could, then she would have the venomous phrase of "*I told you so,*" waiting for him with a smile on her lips. For now, they needed to put the plan in motion. Emerald was counting on them.


*We like being wolves, we do*

*We're in charge and that's for sure*

*We don't take pills to like ourselves*

*In our minds we feel secure*

*We have a social order*

*That is far above the rest*

*We've achieved our status naturally*

*'Cause we know that we're the best*


Amy ventured a look around her Dad's waist, which she knew might well be her last.

"What on earth are they doing, Dad?" Her mouth twisted to one side as she studied the three wolves trying to make sense of it all. "It looks like they want us to throw a ball or something."

"I don't know, Amy" he whispered.

"This is very strange behavior for wolves."

Ken moved his cap forward and scratched the back of his head unable to make sense of it at all.

"At first, I thought they were trying to hold our attention while the rest of the pack snuck around behind us and . . .

This time Amy's voice would have been a low hum if her mouth had been closed, but it wasn't. The tone, loud, high pitched and wavering in the stillness, sounded more like a speeding car trying to skid to a stop before it hit an unmovable object. *Aaaaaaaaaeeeeee* resounded past her lips, spread apart like open castanets. With hands planted over her face, she stared through her fingers into the dark eerie forest behind her, expecting to be trampled by a pack of wolves. Turning, Ken studied his daughter's response with curiosity, for he'd only voiced an opinion, and in his own mind, should not have caused anyone alarm.

"But now, I don't think so," he continued. "I think they want us to follow them."

"I don't think so Ken," Laura wheezed. *How Ken became a forest ranger while disregarding certain facts about animal behavior was beyond her comprehension.*

"I'm surely not that naïve, Ken, to think wolves would act responsibly. Maybe you should read *Little Red Riding Hood* again and refresh your memory as what to expect."

"They just might be trying to help us dear. It's happened before. This could be our only hope."

"We won't be much help to Jamie if those three turn on us…I don't believe in violence, but I'm sure *they* do. Oh, what the heck," she mumbled, waving her hand in the air like she was warding off a swarm of locusts. She wiped the sweat from her brow, even though the night was very cold. She whispered back to Ken through clenched teeth, "okay, okay, *okay Ken!* We'll test them, but only a couple of steps in their direction and see what happens. Why do I get the sinking feeling that soon we'll be the main course?"

Willy wolf was the first to speak, jumping in circles next to his Dad.

*Look Mom and Dad, their coming*

*Though apprehensive fits them well*

*See their faces, see their walk?*

*They're frightened I can tell*

# EMERALD

# *Chapter Eleven*

Emerald, her clan and Jamie, reached the spot down river where the *Northern Bear* gave up its last breath of life . . . where it sank below the cold dark waters, not leaving a trace of her many years of existence. The day had not yet started, but deep gray skies overhead suggested it was laying in wait, as they sat in a circle on the green moss by the riverbank. Jamie was torn between two worlds now. One world was with his parents, sister and friends at school, which now seemed a lifetime ago, though only the course of a single night had passed. Now this new world he never knew existed had drawn him in to be part of their family also. All the close encounters with violence and death had formed a bond between them that would last forever, but sadly only reached by memory. To leave them now was going to be difficult, but he knew it had to happen. *"Just be glad you were able to share their world for a night"* his mind called out. *"Few if any are given such a privilege."*

Emerald brushed a wisp of ebony hair away from her green eyes and focused on her friend. Friend yes, but she had also fallen in love. That was perfectly acceptable as far as feelings went, but that was all that it could ever be and that was sad. A tear fell from her eye onto her cheek and she brushed it away with the pad of her finger. Mother Nature had given her extraordinary powers to be used for one purpose, to make her forest and its citizens safe from harm. *Nothing more.* To use magic for one's own desires was forbidden. Having the gift of magic was awesome and she hoped Mother Nature would be proud of her efforts. Falling in love was not against the rules of behavior, but only if she did not take advantage of it. *Pickles!*

She took a Valla Laun seed from her pouch and placed it in Jamie's shirt pocket. There was a waver in her voice as she spoke, and Jamie could sense her sorrow.

"Jamie, I'm going to miss you more than you will ever know, but I cannot use magic to upset the laws of the universe. Magic is only to be used to improve the odds of a bad situation."

"I *knew* it was only going to be for one night," Jamie began. "I know that time has now come. *Oh bother!*," he exclaimed, as his eyes misted over. "This has been the best time of my life with you and your family and I hope it does not mean goodbye forever, for that would be terrible. *I love you*," he whispered, wringing his hands together, not knowing quite what to do with them. "I've never told a girl that before," he said. He could feel the heat rushing to his face with those few words and knew his ears were turning red. "I always thought those words would be hard to say, but it was not. Not even in front of your family. *Wow*, I can't believe I said that."

"You said what is in your heart and that is what everyone should do. *Believe it*. This isn't forever Jamie, you'll see. A pure heart finds ways."

Jamie hugged Cyra, Luna, Raal, Bolo, Mika, Woon, and finally Emerald, finding it difficult to break away. Emerald kissed Jamie on the lips and his heart melted like warm honey, his face flushing a deep shade of pink. Everyone could tell, but he didn't care. That was a moment he would treasure for the rest of his life. To wash his face would now seem irreverent, after being touched by such beautiful lips.

"Lie down and close your eyes, Jamie," Emerald was saying. He could hear her voice, but his mind had not fully recovered from that remarkable kiss.

"The morning is only minutes away, so we must hurry. There will be a white light and then you will be back in your realm. We'll not forget you. *Ever*."

Emerald touched the silver flute to Jamie's chest and he was enveloped in a ball of silver light. *Whrrrrrrr!*

\*\*\*

It was Willy who saw him first and he jumped in circles around his Mom and Dad, his gleeful high-pitched voice ringing through    the trees.

*Hey Mom, and Dad, they see their son*

*They're running to his side*

*Look how they hug and kiss him*

*I feel warm inside with pride*


*'Cause we found them and we found him*

*And we got them all together*

*If not for us (our cleverness}*

*They'd have searched and searched forever*

Wanda and Wally joined in with their son as they looked on with an air of accomplishment.

*The fairies will be pleased with us*

*This worked well we must say*

*No one was hurt, they found their child*

*As the glow of sun fades night away*


*We like being wolves we do*

*We're in charge and that's for sure*

*We don't take pills to like ourselves*

*In our minds we feel secure*


*We have a social order*

*That is far above the rest*

*We've achieved our status naturally*

*'Cause we know that we're the best*

*Better than the rest!*


\*\*\*

Reluctantly following the wolves for some time, it was Laura who first saw Jamie asleep on the riverbank, just as the sun announced the beginning of a new day. The three wolves turned and disappeared into the foliage, their job done now, as Laura let out a *whoop!* She ran toward her son in wild abandon. There was not a single thought of *wolves* ever crossing her mind, now that Jamie was in sight.

She kneeled next to her son pulling him to her breast.

"Jamie, Jamie, wake up. Oh God Ken, is he breathing?"

Jamie opened his eyes to see his frantic parents staring down in anticipation. It took a moment for his brain to understand it all.

"Oh Lord, are you hurt . . . Did you fall? Jamie? *Jamie?"*

Laura was beside herself with worry as she stroked Jamie's hair with her fingers, waiting for an answer that seemed to take forever.

"No Mom, I was just lost, and . . . "

Ken sighed, putting his arms around Laura and Jamie.

"It's easy to get lost out here. The Rain Forest is a big place to wander off into. Luckily we had help from some beings you would not consider friendly or we might never have found you."

Amy stuck her head in between her parents to stare at her brother.

"Wolves brought us to you. Three of them. It was scary, Jamie. They have gold eyes and ---"

Laura put her fingers against Amy's lips.

"That's enough Amy, we can talk about that when we get home. You must be starved. You're sure you're alright?"

"I'm fine, Mom. Just a little dazed for some reason."

"Here, drink some of this water son," Ken said. "You're probably dehydrated, and that'll make you feel squirrely."

He handed him the canteen and waited as he took a long hard gulp of fresh water. Jamie was quite sure he shouldn't mention spending the night with fairies and elves or being saved from the river's wrath by Emerald. To think of it now, it did sound a bit farfetched. Did it really happen? Now that he was back with his parents, he wondered, could it have been all a dream? *Oh God*, he hoped it was real. But to try and explain it to his family would only prove to them something serious had happened to his mental condition after a terribly dark night in the forest. *Alone*!

"That was the worst storm we've had in the forest that I can remember, Jamie," Ken began.

"Any number of things could have happened to you in the blink of an eye. I'm sure you learned something from this, but we're proud of you for making it through. Now let's get home to a warm fire and a hot meal. You missed your birthday party, but I'm sure the cake is still waiting."

# EMERALD

# *Chapter Twelve*

Jamie sat out under a tree in front of the cabin. It was evening after dinner, and a month had passed since his ordeal in the forest. The next full moon was overhead and drew his mind back to that special time of his life. Torn by what was real and what was not, he wondered, could it have all been a vivid dream? Emerald had not diminished in his mind the way most dreams can in the passage of time, but common sense told him fairies and elves might be better classified under the same fantasy label as Santa Claus and Peter Rabbit. For a moment gloom began to seep into the corners of his mind and he stuck his hands in his coat pocket as a sudden chill overtook him. The fingers of his right hand touched the small necklace given him by Emerald that night in the Grand Hall. *Wow!* He held the beautiful ornament in the palm of his hand and his heart flooded with joy. Emerald was *real*. How could he have doubted it? Why do we always seem to trust what we are told to be the real truth? There are certain moments in our lives that are so grand, they never fall from grace and this was Jamie's finest hour, holding the truth in his hand. Emerald's words, *"We'll meet again,"* surfaced in his  mind as he began to remember dreams that hugged his mind nightly in sleep.

*When you come near*

*When I can see that glow*

*That something that undoes me*

*Steals my heart and . . . Oh!*

*I breathe in deep*

*I want to bathe in that thrill*

*Thrill of touch*

*The night so still*


*In my bed I have*


*Dreams-you are there with me*

*Dreams-in the night I see*

*You real as one could be*

*Stay with me now*


*Your laughter soon will*

*Fill my heart I know*

*'Till that time in*

*Dreams I will go*


*Warm lips brush faint*

*across my cheek I feel*

*The soft breath of love tingles*

*Oh . . . So real*

# EMERALD

*Our spirits meet in dreams*

*I know you are there*

*Rose petals light and fair*

*Scent the air*


*In my bed. . . I have*


*Dreams- you are there with me*

*Dreams-in the night I see*

*You-real as one could be*

*Stay with me now*


*My senses rush I feel my heart . . . Race*

*Then I wake as we embrace*

# *Chapter Thirteen*

Emerald rose early, for this was to be the day to clean the rest of soot and debris left behind in the castle from the ravaging fire. Fixing the water barrel though, was another problem, which was going to take the skill and strength of many elves under the watchful eye of Mika. She walked down the corridor through the open portal to meet the first rays of light shining through the trees. She flew down to the pond to splash fresh water on her face and tie a ribbon in her hair. She suddenly realized flying seemed to be second nature to her now. She smiled at her image in the still waters of the pond, remembering special moments with Jamie. She wished him the best, but oh how she would miss him. With a gentle leap toward the sky, she flew back up to the limb outside her bedroom and found a comfortable spot to sit. The shafts of sunlight were warm and enticing on her bare shoulders, as she breathed in the crisp morning air. Her mind wandered back to that misty morning in the clearing when she became a Princess. She smiled, remembering how awkward she felt with herself. And then, having to face the Goddess of the Olympic Rain Forest, A warm sensation wrapped around Emerald's heart, for she felt Mother Nature was Near. And she whispered, *"Thank you Mother Nature. You touch my soul, my heart. Thank you for the forest, your most beautiful work of art."*

The leaves rustled around Emerald to blend in with Mother Nature's gown, as she suddenly appeared. Sitting next to her Princess, she pulled her close.

"You are welcome. I'm very proud of you. A lot happened in this forest in the course of a single night and you came through like the *Princess* I knew was hiding inside of you. You handled every situation with valor and grace."

"In all honesty Mother Nature, I'm not sure what you saw was really me. When I touch the magic flute, I become someone I don't even recognize."

As she spoke, tiny sparkles brushed from her wings to float above, vanishing in the mist of early morning.

"That is the real you, Emerald. The magic will not work with everyone, but Cyra saw that special light in your heart. Those sparkles you see are a tribute to that. When you speak from the heart, light brushes from your wings, a telltale sign that you are truly princess material. I don't know of any other fairies besides you and Cyra who would experience the rush of magic and connection with the universe by touching the flute. For most, it would just be a flute and some tiny seeds from a very pretty flower. You have earned the title of Princess, Emerald. What you witnessed was the real you." With those words, Mother Nature kissed Emerald, sending a warm fuzzy feeling skidding through her body and her heart thumped. Then, with the same visual softness as her entry, she slowly vanished into the surrounding foliage. Emerald leaned back against a smooth branch and took in a deep breath of crisp morning air, feeling so blessed. If not for Mika saving her from harm's way that fateful day thirteen years ago, so many lives would have been altered. The thought was fascinating. She reached for the flute and pressed it against her lips. The melody seemed to flow from her heart. Life was good.

## *The End . . . For Now*

## ABOUT THE AUTHOR

Lucky Wright grew up in Palos Verdes estates, California. He attended Los Angeles Art Center School College of Design, with an interest in Illustration and Lettering. As a saxophonist, he toured with Chubby Checker, Del Shannon and Bobbie Rydell in a band called the Peppermints, to introduce the "Twist" to the world. It was then he discovered the desire to write. Having raised six children together, Lucky lives in Torrance, California with his wife Phyllis.

www.ingramcontent.com/pod-product-compliance
Lightning Source LLC
Chambersburg PA
CBHW030537130626
46552CB00006B/2300